W H I S P E R S

Dear Dr. Cone little
Enjoy this
Journey
Fleming
Beverly
April 1, 2002

WHISPERS

≋

A Novel for a
New Millennium

BEVERLY J. BELL

Locust Valley Press

New York

Locust Valley Press, Inc.
c/o Bell Winslow
3 Salem Way
Glen Head, NY 11545

ISBN 0-9661748-0-1

This book is affectionately dedicated to Lee,
who was always the first to read it and who was,
throughout, a source of inspiration.

꓂

ACKNOWLEDGMENTS

I must begin by thanking my dear husband, Francis Dana Winslow, who never left my side and who understood that I had to see this project through. His input always kept me focused on my paramount concern, my love for creation and my belief in the equality of all living beings.

I cannot let this book go out without thanking all of those friends who read any number of the drafts, especially the early ones, and who gave me the support to keep editing it. Thank you Dennis Haber, Daren Rathkopf, Jim Eisenman, Steve Conlon, Laura Pinto and Larry Amaturo, to name a few.

To Clarissa Watson and Edith Hay Wyckoff, my partners who launched the project.

To Uncle Ernie who read it and saw a different Beverly and to Aunt Beverly who even composed songs and musical accompaniments for a musical version of the book.

To Diana Alutto whose artwork inspired me to keep working on *Whispers*. She found the hidden typos and just kept reading it and encouraging others to do the same. Diana always believed in the message.

To Fay Roosevelt Fisher, a kindred spirit and gifted teacher who even clarified a passage for me and let me know I was on track.

To Joe Carrieri who walked me through his own publishing journey, *Searching for Heroes*. He helped my dream reach others.

To Genevieve Murray and Virginia Witkowsky who helped me with the many drafts and formats of the manuscript.

To Tom Hogan whose artwork graces my cover.

To David denBoer who walked me through the printing maze, designed the novel and was a source of good counsel throughout the process.

To every man, woman, animal, plant and mineral; your spirits shall inherit the earth and one day we shall all be in harmony.

To all of my readers who will soon start to listen to the Whispers, this little journey is for you.

PROLOGUE

ꝫ God perspired. He took his appointed seat on the dais, pulled out an amber handkerchief and dotted his forehead to remove the droplets peeking out from under his hairline. He arose, made his way to the podium, hesitated and turned away from the multitude. A judgment speech, a determination? Dead silence.

"What are you going to do about this calamity?" a frenzied speaker shouted. "If you know all, you know there is no hope for that place. If you love your creation, you will deal with this in a summary fashion and let us get on with our lives. If you are not all of these, perhaps you should not be up there in the center seat!"

"Nonsense," shouted another. "He is the Master Creator. Where do you get the authority to accuse him of such things?"

"I get it from the consensus gathered here today," was the retort. "Unless you've been somewhere else, or asleep, you know that each and every one of us is in danger of being destroyed by the emanations coming from that place. We came here to act, and, I might add, we all expended great energy to be here. So, let's get on with it. I have it on good authority that the arsenal is in place. That's what we came for. We came to give the final authorization for the release. It'll take a millisecond, and we can all go home."

"Enough, enough!" The Creator silenced them as he reclaimed his demeanor. "We came here for a trial."

"Ialdabaoth, what gives you the right to hurl such epithets?"

"I'm scared. I'm tired. I'm, I'm afraid you are no longer aware."

With this, God rolled his head back, grasped the silver podium, and an aura of blue surrounded his slight frame. He reached down and gave a gentle pat on the head of his mascot, Jeremiah, a jet black cat who by now had wound around God's legs at least five times in his consummate gesture of comfort and comraderie.

"I have an idea," was all God said.

WHISPERS

CHAPTER *1*

꒳   I'm an old Maryland boy born and bred. My father always told me, and his words ring in my memory to this day, "Just plant the seeds in the fertile Maryland earth, and leave all the growing to Mother Nature. She's the kindest farmer there ever was." And so it was the Campbells came over from Scotland and settled here 200 years ago. They farmed the fertile Maryland shore, harvested her corn and soy and watched the spring rains gently sculpt the dense pink clay soil into little islands in oceans of life-giving moisture and nutrients.

By the time I was six I had mastered my dad's tractor and worked on the family farm after school. After high school I decided to break out of the family mold and run a hardware store. There I could dole out, with each and every order, all the seed, fertilizer, and carefully crafted tools for each and every one of my colleagues who was sowing Mother Earth. I am happy with my lot in life. I never went away to college, unlike some of my more illustrious friends. But I get to sit and trade stories with all the other souls who are still planting the seeds, watching for the rains, praying that disease spares their little plot, and hoping that the earth continues to yield those bushels of grain which parlayed into dollars, form the bread of life.

I always believed in the words of my father. They were the same words handed down by his father and his father before him, all the way back to the 1700s. "Mother Nature will always provide." What I was to learn in the summer of 1994 made me rethink trusting Mother Naure's good will to enhance our life style.

God, I love the Maryland farm country around Oyster Cove! You can drive for miles and miles and see nothing but the winter wheat bending in one ceaseless pattern, so much like the waves undulating out on the Chesapeake Bay.

The Chesapeake has a commanding personality as she extends her vast watery life-giving influence in tentacles of bays, inlets and rivulets. These form safe harbors for every form of migratory bird that finds its home on the East Coast. It's such an oddity, I think, that the wild fowl from all over North America settle here in the winter, trying to reclaim the safe dens provided for them through Nature's plan. They are frustrated by the pressure-treated wooden docks so deliberately placed over their habitats. They run for endless feet across the salt marshes and shallows to accommodate the roaring, guzzling badges of wealth which are the ostensible signs of prosperity now sported by the residents here.

It is always natural for the native in any area of our country to ponder the lot of those who move in, transplants from another place, who exhibit their success through the clearing of trees, pouring of monumental foundations and the erection of hulking houses as testaments to their own personalities. However, here in Oyster Cove their presence made me even more uneasy than it should have, I think.

Oyster Cove itself, the commercial and business district, which I call home for so many hours of my day, is considered quite picturesque by these Washingtonians. Row after row of pink brick colonial homes now serve as store fronts for real estate brokers, who eagerly escort the transplanted down our highways and byways to find the rivulet that most pleases them. We have the usual assortment of charming country inns, renovated by the entrepreneurial middle class. They attract the in vogue, upwardly mobile young couples, eager to romp in the beauty of the area for a weekend, to savor the smell of newly made biscuits at ten o'clock on Saturday morning and to trade for Staffordshire dogs and cobalt glass in our local antique shops.

How did such a pristine enclave become the 'Playground of the Eastern Shore'? Twenty miles down the road lies the great arching Bay Bridge. The giant arm connects the shore with the clamoring masses of self-proclaimed earthy business people from Washington and Baltimore as they try to lose themselves in our fields and bays. The bridge was conceived by our planners as the conduit for our development, our great rainbow for the future.

As I watch the unalterable pattern of imported cars, all strikingly similar, metallic light green, blue and white, laden with blonde ladies carefully decked in pastel pants with complimentary T-shirts sporting little pocketbooks with ivory whales, I ponder how our rainbow could have become such a mixed blessing. How could its builders ever have allowed an area such as ours to embrace with open arms those who soon imprinted their designs on our rolling fields of innocent winter wheat and proud corn?

CHAPTER 2

Back home to our all American community came one of our favorite daughters one dusty June Sunday afternoon.

What a homecoming. No Sunday dinner waiting at the table or happy hugs to receive back the hometown girl made good. Elisha Martin's parents were both dead; their old housekeeper had summarily followed. Her sister lived far away, a continent, a world away. No. Elisha returned to Oyster Cove on her own in a dusty little Buick piled to the gills with her clothes, books and cat, Felicity Ann, paraphernalia. Not a grand entrance, but that was in keeping with the mystery of her return.

She purchased a little out of the way, run-down cottage on the outskirts of town. I questioned at first her choice of such a spot. One would think that a bright young minister would choose one of the nice red brick Victorian houses along Main Street, with the white gingerbread and refinished oak doors. Growing up, Elisha had always loved those big old houses. Now, when she seemingly could afford one, she chose an old run-down gray weathered bungalow. Surely she received something substantial from the Martin inheritance. Her Dad had been a chemist for one of the Baltimore pharmaceutical houses, and he always treated his little family to the best of everything. Why also, did she settle outside of town, a place choked with weeds and briars? I was later to understand that even this choice of hers was part of the plan that was unfolding before her, one that I later learned was unknown to her.

I had known Elisha since childhood. We shared many of the same teachers in elementary and high school. I admired her; I guess I loved her from afar, but nothing ever came of it. I talked her through her parents' overzealous supervision of dates and her fear of the SAT's. I even filled in as her date for the Junior Prom when the fellow who asked her lost his heart to a red-headed cheerleader two weeks before the dance. I lost touch with Elisha after high school, but news of her achievements reached me when a few old friends got together over a few beers after work. Good old Mrs. Smithers, an old friend of Elisha's mother, was also a reliable source of information about Elisha's storybook life.

The news about her was all pretty general information. After a distinguished career in college, she went directly to seminary in New Jersey and ended up with a small rural congregation somewhere in the heartland. There she served as Pastor for the last ten years. She never married. Strange for someone so pretty and well adjusted. I had always been in awe of her. How could a pert 5' 2" little bit of a thing, with green eyes as crystal—sharp as the finest tourmaline, master everything she tried and keep that Elisha Martin charm! At once her eyes could burn with the heat of the most passionate lover, yet be as cool and poised as the depths of the deepest Arctic lake. Always a study in opposites, she was sensual and remote, intelligent and a bit silly, feminine and yes, masculine, all at the same time. I guess that scared the men she met along the way. It scared me when we were in high school.

I saw her again when she came into my store to purchase some cleaning supplies for the bungalow. "Hi Will," she said as she fumbled for her purse. Some of her hair fell across her forehead in a way which made her look a bit like Jean Harlow in faded blue jeans.

"Good to see you after all these years. What brings you back to the old stomping grounds?" I asked, eager to draw her out a little. Maybe I would get a better picture from that usually recounted by Mrs. Smithers. I really wanted to find out what in the world made her return to this dull, uninspiring, very regular Maryland village. I had to be stuck here, but there wasn't a reason in the world, as I could see it, for a talented young minister to be here. Who would she talk to, after all? Me? Gosh, all I could do is help her with her cleaning items and recommend the right kind of hasp to attach to the back door.

"I left in a hurry, Will. The Church didn't even have time to give me a farewell dinner or anything. I just told them I was going back home to Maryland, and here I am."

"But what will you do here?" I was sorry I put it so bluntly, but that's me. After all, here was the old flame in my life, and I couldn't even make her feel welcome. She didn't answer me, and I didn't blame her. On reflection, I could see that something stirred within her. Whatever it was was definitely off-limits.

Elisha's return to Oyster Cove gnawed at me. Why at this time? And why couldn't she fill in a few more details? A few days after our visit at the store Mrs. Smithers stopped in. She was always good for a few local stories. She even made a purchase that day. Usually she comes in just to bend my ear. I don't mind; life gets tedious behind a counter if there aren't a few tidbits of gossip thrown in.

"Morning, Mrs. Smithers," I said.

"Good morning, Will. I need some help with my gutters. Do you have some kind of contraption that cleans the leaders to get rid of all the clogged leaves?"

"Sure thing. Come on over here." I led her over to my long plastic pipes and began to fashion a special tool, just the right thing for the job. "Say, have you heard anything about Elisha Martin? She came in here a few days ago. Any read on why she came back?"

"Read?"

"Oh, I'm sorry, just my slang for opinion." I was a bit embarrassed by my free and easy way.

"Well, no, actually. I really don't know why she's back here. I did hear that she had some trouble with a few people in her congregation. You know, Will, you can't please everyone. Anyway, she seems to think she's been untrue to her call. You know how ministers always obsess over their call. . . . Sounds a bit like that to me."

"I don't know. I do know she never fully recovered from the death of her parents," I said.

"Maybe her memories of town are just too strong. If she has to be back here, I guess she'd just as soon start fresh," Mrs. Smithers added.

"Fresh is a way of putting it," I said. "Who in the world would want to live out in that swamp?"

"Not me, I can assure you," Mrs. Smithers answered. "Yes, Will, that will do just fine," she said, motioning to my creation for her gutters.

"That will be $2.50."

"$2.50 it is; see you soon."

She left with pole in hand happier than I had usually seen her. It's simple things that make people happy, like being able to clean their gutters.

Elisha, in spite of all her accolades in high school, always possessed an annoying self-effacing attitude. It was bothersome to me because it kept her apart from all of us. Maybe she thought she could not live up to our expectations. The fact is, they were hers and hers alone. It plagued me because I tried so darned hard to do well and to earn the tickets to college. She did so beautifully so effortlessly, and she drew many compliments.

I remember when she won the award for the best voice in ninth grade. She turned to me when I congratulated her and said, "Sally Johnson studied three years and is the best soprano in this county. Why should I have this award?" I just shrugged and could not understand her response at the time. Elisha had by far the clearest voice, the most moving quality. Why couldn't she feel that? Why did she always feel guilty for being gifted? I think she carried all of that over into her ministry. She underestimated her ability to receive the message and to preach. She could never feel the love of people around her.

I continued to hear from the local gossips that she wasn't doing much of anything back on her place, which she affectionately named 'Whispers'. She would sit for hours in the middle of a sparse thicket of loblolly pine. The mosquitos were intolerable to all of us in that swamp, but she seemed to be content there in those glades, the ladies said. They even heard her speaking out loud to seeming nothingness. I decided it was time to find out for myself just what sort of breakdown she was going through. That would be my mission through the summer of 1994. At least, I thought, someone should tell her that she was becoming the talk of the town, and this time she wasn't the golden girl.

CHAPTER 3

Between the Bay Bridge and Oyster Cove lies the exclusive community of White Marsh. How often I have reflected on the irony of the name. The locale had once been one long undulating field of marsh grass and cattails situated on one of the Chesapeake's deepest, most sheltered harbors. Myrtle Creek was one of the most effervescent arteries of the Bay, carrying ever forward to that great body of water all of the life-giving nutrients that the soils, which support the habitat, gracefully hand over as their dower. As I stealthily sneak past the private police force which guards the entry of the one lane road comprising the main street of this residential village, I know that I am an interloper not welcomed by the residents. I am tolerated, since I am the paid Village Clerk. I keep the records of all meetings, mail notices to all residents, accept complaints from the bored ones who have nothing better to do than to gently tattle on their best friends.

Jutting out over the cattails and mother ducks' carefully constructed nests of local grasses lie the majestic monuments to each resident's masculinity and success. They are easy to spot, one hundred fifty foot long docks, which float as ever present supports for their toys. Each Saturday and Sunday morning the owners, a bit full from their rich breakfasts, climb aboard their cruisers and obtain the thrills of their lives as they allow the gentle summer wind to brush the hair back from their temples. They feel alive and exhilarated. Once their yachting tour is complete, they motor slowly home, careful to be seen by each resident, watchful that every neighbor notes that this boat is not the one from last year but an additional new badge of success. Lest no one notice the changes in color year to year, this is done creatively by naming and renaming the boats Dory I, II, III, IV, and so on as each year the Dory adds on an additional ten feet in length.

Dotting nature's creek are the monuments of glass and steel, which are blithely called home by the residents who live their lives in absolute perfection. They each make certain that there is not one dent on the steel banisters which soar three stories in the air, nor cracks in the Italian tile kitchen floors, so white, so un-stained, they bely their own sterility. To this lovely little haven have come all of the people who 'made it' in Washington and Bal-timore. They made it by shaving ever so slightly the salaries paid their workers, and by aiding each other with innocent tips on their own corporate dealings, facts so blatantly illegally passed, yet so readily accepted by such a genteel bunch.

I have often mused to myself how the White Marsh folk have developed a unique way to give back to the area; they throw char-ity balls. They dance the night away under tents lavished with glorious flowers clutching the center poles for life. The decora-tions are arrayed in profusion. The flowers seem to be railing at the masquerade they are forced to play. So many of them are cut and then twisted into contorted arrangements in an effort to hide the tent poles or wires. Their dying beauty forms the backdrop for the charades played by the revelers.

Some residents give up the use of their homes for a time and turn them over as sites for these grand balls. They are then writ-ten up in glowing detail in all of the local papers. Wherever the dances are held, the band plays into the night, the dresses are all taffeta and poufed, the hair sleek, make-up scant, and the conver-sation is self-congratulatory. Money pours out of these events for all manner of charities. It is the way the people of White Marsh are charitable. They dance. They dance. They dance.

My concern with this tiny example of America at its best, lies not in my philosophical commentary on the mores of the bright and beautiful, but on the fact that that very summer many of my hours were absorbed as Clerk in dealing with one illustrious resident, Jonathan Seward. He had been asked by the Federal Environmental Protection Agency to remove his dock, since it had never received a permit allowing it to invade the mallard's nests and destroy the crabs' bottom home. The Village, embarrassed by this Federal intervention, felt duty bound to exert its own pressure on Mr. Seward. Since I preferred to spend my long evenings at home with a barbecue and a good book, I resented the hours I had to spend at my second job when they competed with the Chesapeake summer.

The immediate problem was that the Bay no longer was supporting some of its cornerstones of life. Last year the master crabbers complained that their yield was substantially lower than that of the previous one. This particular spring showed a marked decrease in the number of crabs finding their way into their wire mesh final resting places. There, indeed, was a sinister change occurring in Chesapeake Bay. It was felt by some of the people in positions of power in Washington, White Marsh and Oyster Cove that the docks were the culprits. The churning of the brass propellers as they slowed their way into their wooden berths changed forever the natural habitat for the crabs. As each dock was crafted, the stiff and sinuous marsh grass was uprooted, and tons of quarried rock installed to give the area a more 'polished look.' Nature had so carefully planted her grasses to attract insects and other bits of food for her water fowl and crabs. Last year's brown stalks became the mothers' nests. Now all that was left was the germicidal, dry, barren, desert-like landscape which was determined to be the mark of success in White Marsh.

I muse so often as I drive along our country lanes between Oyster Cove and White Marsh that all of the carefully planted hybrid flowers and shrubs coveted by the White Marsh residents seem strangely out of place. They are all so evenly placed, mathematically and geometrically planted; even those shrubs with natural uplifting habits are clipped and shorn, squared and rounded, their natural inclination toward the sun held in check. With a diligent hand they lose their reason to be, their beauty, their uniqueness. What a contrast they are to the profusion of color in wild array along the road in the drainage ditches and even bursting through the pavement cracks. Nature scatters her weeds and wildflowers at random and is much more creative at giving us effortless beauty than all of those hours spent trimming, clipping, and pruning shrubbery to fit our own design. How many of my friends delight in the road show, I wonder. How many take off their hats to such a grand performance, indeed.

My father had a good grasp of the White Marsh phenomenon, although in Dad's time he just referred to the people living along Main Street with the polished oak double doors and verandas set with wicker and geraniums as being 'different.'

"You know, Will," he'd say in his inimitable way, "They're not better than we are, just a little more blessed. It's how they use their blessings that makes them special or not."

Dad was one of Old Maryland's best. The soil lived in him; he was a part of it. He never really told me what he meant by special, and I never really asked him. I should have, though. Looking back on it now, I know he had more insight than most. But is 'special' the word? I don't really know myself.

The officials decided that the first docks to be targeted were the ones for which not even a modicum of attention to local regulations had been given, those docks which were stealthily placed by the people who felt that the law was never intended to be the set of rules within which they had to live. They, who controlled so many people's lives, had the right to control the Bay.

And so it was with Mr. Seward who was called to task by his peers, the Board of Trustees of the Village of White Marsh, one early June evening that year. The Mayor, Jason Smathers, who was descended from the early farmers who used to till the fragrant valleys of White Marsh, was eager to appear in control. He called the meeting to order. I, of course, was still fiddling with my tape recorder, which was, on that night, particularly bothersome. A darting, reproachful glance from Mayor Smathers let me know that the provincial joking about my inefficient equipment was inappropriate at this point. Singular changes were to be made, and the focus was to be on them.

When the Calendar was called, Jason Pratt, a senior Trustee, immediately launched into his carefully prepared speech. "Mr. Mayor, not only do I find the handling of this matter grossly inadequate, but I am here to place on the record the fact that what we have here is a flagrant violation of the regulations."

Mr. Pratt neglected to say on the public record that he had recently been denied membership at the local yacht club due to a letter written by Mr. Seward. In his brilliant and committed execution of his civic duties, he was now seeing to it that his next door neighbor lost the delightful right to traverse marsh lands which he, happily, still enjoyed. His angular face which had frightened so many back in Washington, where he had been the chief contractor for all of the sewers in the downtown business district, puffed with his importance.

I mused to myself that this was the commitment and competence which I had viewed for so many years in my position as Village Clerk. The Village boasts a census of two hundred. The issues addressed are generally minor. Nevertheless, they require sincerity and focus. I had learned to expect to see the meetings as merely battles over petty neighborhood grievances and embarrassments. I wondered if this occurred in all of villages and towns which dotted the beautiful coastline of the Maryland I still loved.

The next comment, that of Trustee Morgan Turnbull, was directly to the point. Covering his mouth gently with his right hand to muffle the comments on my recorder, he remarked, "Seward lured my caretaker away for a dollar more an hour just after Easter. I had a wedding planned for the month of June, and everyone knew that. It's a damn shame when we start stealing each other's servants. That sort of thing just isn't done. Now, that says a lot about a man like Seward."

"That's right, I heard the same story from Edith Hightower. We all work together around here to keep the salaries consistent. It's hard to find good people," the Mayor added.

"It's hard when you have people like Seward around," Turnbull sneered. "Let's get him out of here."

The cacophony, which had long become the symphony of Trustees' voices to me, continued. Each recounted his story of similar social faux pas committed by Mr. Seward. So engrossed in themselves in their eagerness to promote their own positions, they soon lost sight of the fact that they had met to prevent another nail in the coffin of the Bay. They continued the onslaught on Mr. Seward's character well into the wee hours of the early morning. I was thankful that I had used the tape recorder in the discharge of my duties as clerk. I would have given up taking the minutes on this meeting long ago.

As I drove home after the hearing, I stopped at my favorite place, which I frequent at those times when my mind is full and my heart heavy. As I sat gazing over the broad Chesapeake, so calm and quiet in the early hours of the morning, something sharp and rough brushed my moccasin. I looked down and picked up a young crab floating lifeless on its back across the surface of the water. No side stepping jocular entertainer of the deep he; no. He would not even be a meal for a patron down at the Crab Claw in town. His lifeless body was a testament to the past six hours I spent at the Village Hall.

The following day, upon getting wind of the meeting and the intended agenda, Mr. Seward addressed the following letter to the Mayor and the Board of Trustees.

GENTLEMEN:

I find it hard to believe that you would take such an inappropriate action against someone as prominent as I. I paid $6,000,000.00 for the home in which I live, and I have every right to have a dock out to the Bay. I currently operate one fifty foot cabin cruiser, one Boston Whaler, and one sail boat and have every intention of doing so in the future.

I plan to initiate a counter suit against you for $25,000,000.00 for the emotional anguish which you have caused me in this matter, and I plan on continuing to maintain my dock in its present location.

Since there are presently existing numerous other illegal docks in this Village, it is clear that you are embarking on a selective enforcement campaign. Such action is blatantly illegal.

All future correspondence should be forwarded to my attorney. I shall do the same.

Sincerely yours,

Jonathan Seward

No further action was taken by the Board for the rest of the week. The poor Mayor, helpless and ineffectual, the Trustees with no self-control and no self-discipline, all clearly forgot that the Bay they loved was dying with each hour of their lethargy. I mused on how the residents of White Marsh strove for consistency and quality of life. They felt that it was for them and them alone. Strange, people who are entrusted with such important duties resemble nursery school children. If I had held a mirror up to their faces, would they have seen their folly?

CHAPTER 4

℁ Mother Nature treated us all with a familiar June downpour one afternoon. I drove along the narrow lane to Elisha's house, and the ditches were almost full after such torrential rain. I wondered if my surprise visit to Elisha would be welcomed or whether I would receive her now customary rebuff as I had in the store. The road no longer had the hot summer mirages to entertain and transport me. Warm, steamy fog rose, forming ghostly figures, which defied me to chase them with my car. They had their familiar odor of mustiness combined with the gentle fragrance of foliage doused with rain. I love the humid creatures of the thunderstorm. They seem to have a personality as they rise from the asphalt, curling and swaying and beckoning.

Elisha's bungalow was a mile off the main road down a dusty clay-packed lane. After the storm the dust had been treated to a momentary bath, and the puddles in the ruts of the road splashed up under my car as if welcoming me. Funny, I thought, that water should be such a companion and inspiration on this excursion.

I must have driven right by her as I headed to her front door. It took me half an hour to find her after I walked onto her property. As I came up behind Elisha, I startled her. She leaped up from her cross-legged sitting position in the middle of a fragrant loblolly pine glen. Her eyes had been closed ever so gently, and she seemed remote as I approached, as if summarily summoned back, jolted from a journey to a very pleasant place.

"Wow! You gave me quite a start there, Will."

"Sorry, I didn't mean to intrude on your privacy. I just thought I'd come down and see if you needed a little company," I managed to answer.

"Well," she said as she leaned back in a long, rather self-assured posture, "I really wasn't alone, you know."

I looked a bit startled at this answer since I wanted desperately not to believe that the rumors in town about her questionable mental stability had any truth to them.

"No. What I meant was," she continued, "Ty and I were just having a grand old time comparing our notes on the storm and what the storm means to each of us."

The conversation by now was getting a little weird even for a good old sport like me.

"Okay, Elisha. You know, perhaps you feel that you can trust my being open about some of your idiosyncrasies. I think you'd better be aware that I'm still the same guy that you left here after you graduated. I'm pretty dense when it comes to your having discussions with the air."

"Oh no, Will," she mused, "I'm not discussing these beautiful things with myself." As she said this a serenity came over her face, and with her right hand she brushed back her bangs. She was the most beautiful woman I had ever seen.

"Come here, Will." She summoned me with a little clap of her hands and asked me to sit down next to her, right there in the middle of the glade. "Close your eyes, Will. Sit here next to me. Just close your eyes and clear your mind of all your thoughts. Clear your mind of how many orders you filled today or how many people complained because you have the wrong size door-mats in stock. Sit down. Just take a deep breath and smell the essence of the pine."

Well, I have to admit it felt a little funny sitting cross-legged in the middle of the woods with my old friend, taking in familiar smells and feeling that I would get anything out of it. I went along with the whole thing anyhow, and I sat there for almost an hour with her. We did not speak, but I felt a tranquility that I hadn't known since the exhilarating feeling I used to get Friday afternoons when school was out so many, many years ago. I remembered. The thought of two days off was the greatest thing in the world. It was a sort of peace, a freedom from the week's relentless monotony. I felt the same release that evening. I didn't tell Elisha much about how I felt. After a time, I got tired of scratching my ankles, since the mosquitos were worse at dusk when the sun ceased protecting us humans from their annoying stings.

"I'll see you around, Elisha. I just thought you probably needed some company," I said as I shook her hand and looked into those cool green eyes.

"I'd love to have you come back again, Will," she mused, "But don't worry, I'm not lonely out here."

As I drove back, that strange serenity seemed to last for about ten minutes of the drive. Then as I moved farther and farther away from that quiet glade of loblolly pine, I began to have the same anxiety about Elisha and her questionable return as I had when I embarked on this little misadventure.

The next day after closing up the shop I decided that I would again pay a surprise visit to Whispers and my old friend. As I drove down her driveway, now once again familiarly dusty and gritty on this evening of the longest day of the year, I passed by our glade where we spent our last visit and saw that she was not there. I pulled the car to a halt in front of her weathered gray bungalow. She was sitting rather expectantly on her white wicker chair on the front porch. After she heard the whir of my car's engine as I came to a stop, she leaped up as though she expected me at that very hour.

"Hi there, Will," Elisha said as she greeted me. "Ty told me you'd be here about now, so I fixed you some iced tea with some of the mint from out back."

I was startled by this Ty person. Who was he? I recalled that she had mentioned him in passing the day before. Was he some strange lover she had secretly hidden and brought back from Iowa to keep her company and away from all of us? Or was he some acquaintance that she'd made since she had been here? Strange name I thought, Ty. I didn't know of any in Oyster Cove. This I had to see. As I walked to the back, admittedly I felt a bit intrusive. If she did have a friend here, I'm sure he was already jealous after our sojourn in the loblolly pine glade yesterday.

Elisha was brimming with excitement and anticipation as she took my hand and had me summarily seated in the chair next to her.

"Yes, Ty told me that you got a lot out of yesterday's quiet time and that you would be back."

"So where was he when all of this was going on?" I blurted out. I felt sorry that I'd let some of my unacknowledged jealousy come through as I assaulted her with my questions. "What was he doing, peering at us from behind the pine trees?"

"Oh no," she answered rather quietly, "He was right there next to you the whole time."

At this point I was beginning to feel a number of emotions running the gamut from uneasiness at being in the presence of a crazy woman, to pity for her apparent descent into insanity. I think that the overwhelming pity I felt for her kept me from running straight back to my car and back into town never to be seen at Whispers again. Instead, I let her continue.

"No, Silly. Ty has decided to live here with me for the summer rather than at any of the other places where he could have chosen to alight."

Alight, I thought. That was an interesting word. Who ever talked about a lover alighting at a locale?

"Close your eyes Will. Close them like you did yesterday and take all those crazy thoughts about my being deranged out of your mind. Just close your eyes. Sit here next to me and hold my hand."

This was getting stranger as it progressed. I wanted to hold her hand. By why would she want me to sit there with her if her lover was going to be rounding the corner at any minute, eager to put an end to this interloper? I have to say, I'll never know what kept me sitting in that wicker chair next to my dear old friend, but I did as she requested. I closed my eyes and let my head fall back. I began to float into that reverie that I had felt only a few precious hours earlier.

After about five minutes of what seemed an endless stream of thoughts, reeling through my mind, vision after vision, I became aware of a tingling feeling all over my legs. It was a caress, but more gentle than the sweetest touch I could ever remember. I felt uneasy with my eyes shut so tightly, even though the calm and dreamlike state was beginning to be very enjoyable for me. I opened my eyes, closed them, and then opened them again with the rapidity of gun fire. I could not believe what stood before me. A being swathed in a blue, filmy gauze-like silk toga stood before me and smiled into my face with eyes of pure amber. The face is so difficult to describe, since it was both male and female all at once. It had the fine chiseled nose and beautiful soft eyes of a woman, yet the angular strongly set jaw of a man with long straight golden hair down to its waist. Slowly it extended its hand, reaching into mine, and as I looked down, I saw its feet were unshod.

"Don't be afraid. I know this must be giving you quite a shock." A voice, the softest, most serene voice I had ever heard, spoke those words. All at once I realized that my initial reaction to jump away and to leave forever was assuaged by the cool wash of this voice so full of love. I was transfixed there, more frightened than I had ever been in my life and yet more eager than ever to understand this being before me.

"I'm Ty, Will. I'm the Nature Spirit for the Bay, and I've come here this summer to be with Elisha."

This was getting stranger by the minute. Who and what is a Nature Spirit?

In answer to my unspoken questions he replied, "I'm a Deva, Will. I am a nature guardian, the source and collective consciousness of the Bay. All of the water, all of the rain which falls around the Bay, all of the water which collects in those muddy little puddles after each rain I am. I'm also there in those wispy ghosts that you love to see come up off the asphalt after each storm. I delight in your antics with them. I was amused when you considered them to be ghostly figures. They are, you know, Will. They are just what you were imagining them to be. They are living and breathing as part of me. And those little puddles in the corn fields, they are too. We all answer to our Master Creator, of course. You have heard of the Master?"

Oh, God, this was getting to be too much for me. I looked at Elisha and back again to Ty, and she said nothing. She just smiled up at him as if she'd had this conversation a thousand times and was delighted that some other human being was finally getting a bit of the information.

"Isn't it exciting, Will?" she said as she glanced back at me.

"Well, I don't know about that Elisha. I think its damn strange if you ask me. Here I thought you had some strange friend living with you. Now I find out that he's stranger than strange could ever think of being."

"I'm not living with her," rebuked Ty. "I'm teaching her and living within her. I talk to her throughout the day, in her own thoughts. I have other business in these parts, Will. I don't simply hang around and play tag among the pine trees with Elisha. I am giving her food for thought. She needs this rejuvenation since she questions how she can ever preach again after losing faith in the meaning of the Word."

Well, I could tell that it at least seemed to understand some of Elisha's motivations, but the rest of the speech of this, I don't know what to call it, being, seemed more than I could tolerate. As I started to get up, I felt a strong sense of being pushed back in my chair; yet Ty had moved no closer and no farther away than he had been when he first announced his presence.

"I think you've had enough for today." He turned toward Elisha. "I think he's had enough, Elisha. It's time I left for a few hours."

With this, I felt a warm tingling through my whole body. My head rolled back, and with an inestimable gust of wind, he was gone. I turned to my old friend and said, "What's going on, Elisha?" What truly could be going on that I would see something this fantastic?

"Oh, Will, you know why you're here, and you know who Ty is."

"I do?" I sputtered, falling over the words. "This is amazing. For someone who had so much in common with me, Elisha, I no longer feel that I know you one iota."

"Oh, yes you do, Will, and you know Ty also."

At this, I felt that I could no longer tolerate the once pleasant surroundings of this remote and quiet bungalow.

"I'll catch you on the fly somewhere, Elisha," I mumbled as I dashed to my car.

As I drove down the lane, I remembered that it had been dusty and gritty as I drove up, but now my tires were awash with mud as they rolled through one puddle after another until I reached the main road. Route 50 was as dry as it had been when I entered. I drove home that night not knowing how I got there. I fell into my solitary bed and dreamed of nothing.

CHAPTER 5

≋   I walked in a daze the following day. Somehow I managed to fill everybody's order and advise on the type of paint required for the tasks brought to me. I tried not to think of the events of the previous evening, and yet, for some inexplicable reason, I was comforted by them. I was not as frightened as my conscious mind would lead me to believe I should be.

I returned to Elisha the following evening. As I drove down her lane, I reminisced at how different my feelings were toward her today, this evening, from those of only a few days before. I had come to renew an old acquaintance and to possibly find out why she had become so reclusive and quiet upon her return to her old home. However, now I sought her out as something more than I ever imagined. Her story intrigued me. It felt comfortable to me. That is all I knew.

As I pulled up to the porch, Felicity sat staring out into the fields in her typical Egyptian cat pose. As many times as I have seen it, it always fascinates me to see cats pull their forearms close into their furry underbellies so straight, as though they were performing on the balance beam, so perfectly regal and beautiful. Dusk was beginning to fall again, that grainy dusk, which makes details hard to discern and larger visions much more clear. Felicity's eyes were a dark obsidian color, windows allowing the evening with all of its details to enter her. Her eyes belied what they truly were, black pools of knowledge and understanding. When I looked into them, I sensed that she knew a lot more about what was going on than any human being could ever imagine. I remembered seeing obsidian eyes in another place, but for the moment I could not remember where. I strode toward the front door to find Elisha already there, waiting for me, composed and elusive at first.

"I thought you'd never come back here after what you experienced last night."

"I want to talk to you more about what I saw. I'm not afraid. I may never have left Oyster Cove, but I do some thinking on my own. It may surprise you that I'm not afraid of what I saw."

"Good," she said. "I hoped that you would come back so that we could sit and get to know each other again. There are a lot of things going on in my life, and I want to share them with someone. Until last night I didn't think that anyone would be willing to listen, or courageous enough to believe in what they saw around here."

"Well, I wouldn't go around giving me any medals for bravery. I was just a little worried about you, that's all." I quickly brushed her off. She was getting a bit too close to some of the real fears and concerns I had about the spectacle to which I had been treated last night.

"Sit down, Will," she said calmly, as she poured me some iced tea with a spritely sprig of now familiar mint plucked from her garden patch at the side of the house. I could tell that, through all of her conversation, she had a great need to get to the roots of her life as she had come to know it.

"I had a dream, Will, a dream that Christian ministers are not supposed to have. At the time it occurred I was involved with a million problems within the congregation. Money was tight. We weren't able to pay our apportionments, and there were rumblings that some people were not happy with my preaching subjects. It was a particularly low time for me, and as always, I prayed for guidance. One night I dreamed a dream that for some reason seemed more real than any other dream in my life. It wasn't as surrealistic as some wild, crazy dreams that some people have. It seemed that I was actually in another place dealing with the characters in the dream. Paradoxically, it was the most fantastic, unbelievable vision that I had ever had in my life, and it was more so because I seemed to be living it."

At this point I found that I had sat back in her rocking chair and began, I must admit, listening to the creak and thud of the rocker rails against the uneven floor boards. I'd heard people discuss their dreams before. I'd had some wild ones myself, with people changing locations in the blink of any eye, meeting up with others I've never met before. I thought she was making a little too much of all this, but as a friend I continued to fix my attention on her. She seemed almost breathless to tell me. She had built this up into what seemed to be quite a suspenseful story, suspenseful to her, but not to me. I just sat and gazed with my wide-eyed, generally good-natured appeal.

"Well, remember I told you that I really questioned my ability to lead this particular congregation? You know, Will, I believe there is a time in your life that if you feel you have fulfilled your mission here, you can will yourself to go back to Spirit. I know this is contrary to Christian doctrine, and I don't talk about it with very many people, but I had begun to wonder if it was time for me to go back. After all, ten years in one place without much to show for it, except a few grumbling members complaining behind my back, didn't really inspire me.

"I lay down one night exhausted, not really looking forward to the next day of the same repeated malaise and feeling blue. I closed my eyes, and I guess I dropped off to sleep. The next thing I remembered, and this is the strange part about it, I was standing in what seemed to be a tidal woodland glade with a canopy of tall pine arching up over me. I could see there were no lower branches; the foliage grew only at the top, which formed a firmament between me and the rest of the sky. It was dusk. I could barely see beyond the immediate undergrowth, and it all seemed rather damp and misty. For some reason, I sat down on a seat furnished to me by one of the old pines that had fallen years ago and had allowed itself to be covered over with moss, giving itself back to the earth. Immediately, I became aware that, although I seemed alone in these woods, I was there for a meeting. I don't know how to explain it, but I felt a presence around me. It was beginning to unnerve me, and as I looked around, I glanced to my left. There appeared an almost imperceptible bluish light that didn't seem to have any form. It seemed to be just a breath of baby blue. It was the same blue that you see on infants' coverlets for little boys, or the blue of a forget-me-not petal, very light, very airy. The light seemed to be jumping all around from log to log in a rather methodical yet hapless, ecstatic playfulness. I kept looking at this amazing phenomenon, and as I looked closer it seemed to change from its blue formless, nothingness into the likeness of a crab, you know, the kind of crab that crawls sideways on the ocean bottom. As I looked closer and closer, it seemed to go formless and blue again. There was a feeling of unbridled happiness about it, an almost youthful abandon as it moved from place to place all around me.

"This seemed to go on for about ten minutes when a second light appeared. It was like a green wind, just a breath of green in the air. It swirled in cyclone fashion right at my feet. It began picking up layers of leaves and pine needles which had fallen over the years, and finally dug into the sandy loam beneath. As hard as it is to describe, Will, it was like a little green tornado, and on top of that, it had the distinct odor of pine needles, you know, the balsam kind they use in the pillows they make up in Vermont and upstate New York. It smelled exactly like that. So picture this, Will. There I was in the middle of the glade, a place I'd never been before, with a specter of blue light jumping to and fro and this little green tornado at my feet. They were clearly content and not afraid to be near me, and yet I had no idea what they were or why I was seeing them.

"As I pondered this in my dream, miraculously the answer came to me. From far away I could see another light coming toward me. I know now that it was Ty, Will. It was the same light that I introduced you to yesterday. In the dream, I can't remember if I was afraid. I just stood there and watched this as if I were in a play, staged right before my eyes. The new light, so bluish white, came to within five feet of me and then materialized into the being that you saw yesterday. I don't need to tell you what a fantastic appearance he makes. He spoke to me in his modulated and very middle tone, not male, not female, not high, not low.

"He said, 'You've just seen another Trinity, another way of life, Elisha' and I thought, 'Yes this really is what it's like to be dreaming something.' I was upset about my handling of various subjects in my sermons lately, but what a fantastic manner for my doubts to take shape, in this dream."

I sat gazing at my old friend and wondered if she had been able to make any sense out of such a vision. In response to my unasked question and my silent musings, she spoke softly.

"That's just the beginning, Will. During the course of the next few days after that dream, I had a number of similar appearances, especially of Ty. At first, they occurred only when I went to sleep, but as the days wore on, I grew very listless and uncomfortable in my office or on visitation calls to some of the church members. I find myself lapsing into reveries, or I went back to the glade and met with Ito, the spirit of the crab, as he later told me, Una, the spirit of the loblolly pine, and Ty, though I never remembered most of the encounters. It seemed that I was able to summon them at will wherever I was. I also came to know them, their personalities, their joys, their little quirks, their peeves. It's hard to explain, but through these reveries, I became aware that they were three very special Nature Spirits, guardians of their species. You know, Will, every form of plant, animal, and mineral has its own spirit guide that can materialize at will and direct the destiny of that species. That destiny may even include extinction. They can will that, too."

I began to feel uncomfortable with all of this talk. After all, the only other conversations I remembered having with Elisha centered around her feelings about this and that teacher or her need for a surrogate date for the prom. I had never discussed theology or her beliefs with her. She was a Christian minister, after all, and I never even discussed this aspect of her life with her. Yet, as she recounted these reveries, her eyes danced with a brightness and anticipation that I had never seen in her or for that matter, in any other person. It was this excitement, and only this, which persuaded me to continue to talk to her over a second glass of iced tea.

"The visions became so real that I soon began a regular dialogue with them, just as we are talking. Sometimes I would physically hear the words of the three, and sometimes just the thoughts and answers to my questions would come to mind. Over the next several months I became aware that I was destined to leave Iowa and return home although I had no reason to do so. I could not, for the life of me, understand why it was so urgent that I come home. The understanding that this had to be was as strong as any I had ever experienced.

"So, Will, early one morning I packed up my things, put the cat in her box, and we drove East, back to the Bay. I've had numerous letters from the church members. I know that I could never make amends or apologize enough for leaving the way I did. It would be impossible to make them understand that my move was more important, yes, truly much more urgent, than their immediate need for a new pastor. It is this knowledge that makes things so difficult for me, since I still do not understand why these urgings became so insistent. I know that as a result of my treatment of the congregation, I will probably never obtain another position within my denomination. Still, I know that I did the right thing."

"How do you know what the right thing is, Elisha?" I asked her injecting myself for the first time into the conversation.

"I'm meant for something different, Will. You don't know what it's like out there. I went to seminary and started to think. Then I found myself in a pulpit. Forget about what my sermons said. All I ever heard was, 'Elisha, why don't you cut your hair, dear? You're such a pretty girl, and all that hair makes your face too long,' or 'Why did you let Jim Wierdsma give the roofing contract to his son-in-law? He's just spoon feeding him out of the church coffers, or don't you know that?'"

Elisha halted, "I mean, Will, I mean, who needs all of that? Would you put yourself through it?"

I remained silent. She needed an ear. I could see that. Anyway, I'm just a hardware store owner. What do I know about the ministry?

"Are you listening to me?" she prodded. "Or are you getting distracted again, thinking of something else? I'm here because I need a friend, Will. We always talked back in high school. Please, what do you think? What's wrong with me? I can't even get a response from you!"

At this I picked up my glass and eased halfway out of my chair ready to leave. That's it; I'd had enough.

"Well, what was I going to do? They don't know how to talk to people. That's their problem. I should have known they'd never accept an Easterner anyway, let alone one trained at a liberal seminary. They'll get what they deserve for being abrupt and cold. I know; they'll get another preacher who'll give 'em all the redemption and salvation harangues they want. As for me, as for me, I'm spent for now. Don't you think so—Will? Say something! What am I doing, talking to the wall? I thought of all people, you would understand. Okay, just go back to your little store with all your little patrons bending your ear over the quality of their One-Wipe Dust Clothes, which, I might add, have deteriorated over the years. Go ahead, be my guest."

At this point, she seemed to gaze out over the weedy fields of blue and yellow flowers. For the first time during this meeting she had nothing to say. It was time for me to go. I eased away from her, down the porch steps, and back to town. No good-bye; no 'See ya tomorrow.'

CHAPTER 6

℁ Elisha lay back on her bed of summer mown grass and looked up. The sky was the blue of the bluejay's breast, almost too perfect to be true, but aren't most things which catch our eyes? Ty appeared out of the corner of her right eye as she lay there. The hem of his robe brushed her cheek as he descended from the place where he retreats.

"I missed you. Where have you been?" Elisha asked.

"You know I've asked you to resist that persistent urge to follow my comings and goings. But, I'll forgive you this time. You look tired."

"Tired, I don't know. More like frustrated and bored. I've been hanging around here all week wondering what I'm going to do next."

"Why not try a walk?"

"Do I really look so pale, Ty? It bothers me that I've started looking like that."

"No, Elisha, I only made the remark out of caring, not criticism."

Elisha stared at him for a time, questioning. Her hand found his, so gentle a touch, so warm, almost like it wasn't there but unmistakably present all at once.

"Come with me," he said. He lifted her up to meet him and clasped her hand firmly in his. Slowly they rose above the grass until they were gliding toward Jackson's field a foot above the ground.

"Will I fall?"

"Not if you fight your fear."

"I'm crazy about you, Ty."

Ty said nothing. He continued moving higher and higher over the fields of soy and millet.

"You know, Elisha, I can't let emotions get in the way of the mission."

"Mission?" she asked.

"Emotions," he replied. "Emotions blocking my ability to convey the facts necessary for you to commence your battle. I must watch this. There is a good greater than the good between us. I must remember why I'm here."

"I'm feeling kind of tired. Do you still want to go somewhere?" Elisha interjected.

"You see, emotions can be positive if they don't get in the way." Ty would not be deterred.

"On second thought, maybe I'm not so tired. Where were you taking me?" Elisha demurely slipped her right hand in Ty's left.

"No, Elisha, don't deliberately try to get me off the track." She kept her hand firmly in his. "Come on, all right. Okay, I've got an idea."

"When did you not have one?" she asked.

"A number of times. There are moments when I allow my mind to rest."

"Oh, when? When you are asleep?"

"No. I think you'd be very surprised to know that the only way I can move around the way I do is when my mind is completely void of any focused thought. The pulls of the physical can only be overcome in an unfocused, unattached state."

"So, you're obviously not in an unattached state now." She giggled looking down at her slender hand in his.

"That's it. This is all just too funny for words—is that it? Well, Elisha, just for that, come on—we're leaving for awhile. And forget that tired bit—we're leaving."

"So I see you've been picking up on some of our sayings. I never heard you say 'bit' before."

"Well, you unnerve me when you act as though we were two friends out here on a lark."

"Aren't we?"

"Never."

"Never?"

"Never," he mocked her with his brevity. Ty more than anything fought feelings. The intellectual journeys of the soul were far more appealing.

The atmosphere changed as he drew himself back to the more comfortable realms, his 'reason to be here' goals. These were far more familiar. All of this talk about feelings and the future—well, that was just scary turf.

"Come with me. Come sit on this rock." Ty pointed to an old granite slab imbedded with glistening flaky mica, the kind of rocks guarded by all manner of critters from snakes to centipedes.

Elisha blushed, "I've been too impulsive, haven't I especially for a minister."

"Nonsense, Elisha. Don't resent the fact that I want to change the subject. I just had an idea; that's all."

"After all this time, Ty, I've learned to trust that if you have an idea, we pretty much ought to go with it."

The clouds of the Chesapeake summer afternoon began to form. There are two kinds of afternoons down here. Either they are brilliant sun with nowhere to hide or the high clouds collect to form an overcast, a shield, yes, but also a pall over the afternoon. This was one of those latter types. Elisha could feel the melancholy roll in with each minute. Where did that elated morning rush go?

"Time's up," Ty allowed Elisha a moment's rest and rose, beckoning for her hand. "Time to move away from your fuzzy thoughts."

"What do you mean? Can't I lie back and enjoy the warmth? I was out in the Midwest so long, I'm still cold."

"Your rest is important, but your education more so."

"I'll bet you don't know how drab it gets out there."

"You'd be surprised."

"Oh, would I?"

"Yes. Close your eyes."

"Okay, here we go again. You're great at cutting me off."

"Don't be so sure, Miss Martin."

Elisha shut her eyes. She felt the red warmth under her lids which by now was so familiar. It soothed her. She had been here before. In a millisecond her feet were above the grass; she could just make out the yellow manes of the dandelions. Then she soared higher and higher, her hand held firmly in Ty's until she could no longer make out the frame of her little house.

"I'm scared, Ty."

"I'm confident you are ready," Ty replied.

The two continued to rise until they pushed effortlessly through the bank of clouds which lingered above the Chesapeake. Mile after mile soon placed the two wanderers far above Mother Earth. They were moving faster now, faster and faster until Elisha screamed.

"I'm fainting, Ty!"

"Summon Huron, summon Huron!" Ty shouted to her.

It was too late. Elisha let her head fall back until she lost consciousness.

"Huron! Huron! For God's sake, look at what is happening! Come on, where are you?" Ty shouted.

The next sound was the furious roar of white wind which engulfed the two. Tendrils of white found their way to Elisha's mouth, then opened it, then poured into her mouth the white wind. It filled her lungs, and she started to gasp and to pant.

"More pneuma, more pneuma," Ty shouted. "She is failing; she's choking."

The wind responded. More tendrils caressed her temples and gently entered her nostrils and slid into her lungs. Elisha stirred. Her hands found her face, and she held her temples. Her eyes opened at once.

"Ty, Ty, what's happening to me? I'm sick."

"Just hold on. We're helping you."

She held onto his hand and searched Ty's eyes for some meaning.

"What's happening? I can't feel anything!"

"PNEUMA, come on, move," Ty shouted. The wind became even whiter and enveloped the wisp of Elisha from her head to her feet.

As quickly as it began Elisha ceased trembling and let go of her fear. "I'm feeling better now. It's okay," she moaned. "Where am I?"

"In Shamar."

"Where is that?" she stammered. "Last I knew, I was home on the grass."

"That was the last you knew," Ty replied.

"Where is Shamar?" she persisted.

"It is within an inch of our grasp; it is a billion miles away from Mother Earth. From Shamar we can view our world from afar, and yet we are still within it. It is everywhere; it is far away. We see ourselves. We see all other entities fashioned by our Creator at the time of the great beginning.

"From here, Elisha, your initiation truly commences. I think you will be ready for what I have to reveal to you. Take a moment and look around. Get adjusted to being in a place few alive on your planet ever visit and remember. Of course, as you and all of them dream, you often cross the River and end up here, although the washing afterwards removes all of your memories of it.

"The washing in the water of the River prepares you for re-entry into the physical. It is one of the cruelest things which the Creator does to you."

"Why cruel?" Elisha asked.

"Don't you think it's cruel to give one minute and then take away the next?" Ty continued, "Let me try to be more specific. When you dream, you are often able to connect with old friends, family members, all manner of individuals even from your distant past and memories. You are given insight; you gain perspective on problems of the day—usually the day immediately preceding the dream. How many times have you felt in your dreams that you have actually come to terms with a problem or understood the subtleties of an innuendo?"

"All the time," Elisha interjected. "All the time, and then when I wake up, I can't remember a thing about it."

"Exactly," chimed Ty.

"What?" she asked.

"Exactly. You can't remember a thing about it. The guidance evaporates. What seemed in your dream to be effortless resolution of a problem ends up being forgotten and out of reach. The sad part is the answers are all there, but the wash in the River puts blinders on again."

"Is this water like any other water?" Elisha asked. "Are we talking about a different kind of water? When is water different? You know, maybe this is all too much for me." Elisha tried to move away from Ty, but she could not make one foot move in front of the other. She was paralyzed.

"I can't even get out of here," she screamed. "Let me go! I want to go back home!"

"Are you sure?"

"Yes."

"You're there."

"I'm what?" Elisha looked down, and her feet touched the green grass of her backyard. Her cabin was ahead of her, and Ty was by her side.

"I'm home. That's better," she said.

"Why do you think this is better?"

"Because I can get a grip on my life here. This place is my home. I'm afraid; I'm afraid to be up God knows where."

Ty cut her off. "You can feel secure in Shamar too. In fact, you do when you go there every night. You go willingly. I've even heard you. You call out to deceased family members during the day, and you ask them to join you that night to help you. Be honest. You have done that, haven't you?"

"Yes." Elisha replied.

"Yes, and what makes you so sure I brought you any place different?"

"Because I was conscious—and—and you were there."

"So I'm not supposed to be in your dreams with you?"

"I guess so."

"Elisha, I've got news for you. I've been with you on and off in your dreams for Oh, let's see, the past four or five thousand years or so."

"Ty, I've really got to change the subject or ask you to leave or something. Maybe it has all just been too much—our time travels, your dreams—maybe I need some time off."

"If you had time to spare, I would give you time off, but there just isn't any."

"Why is everything always so urgent with you?"

"Because it isn't with you."

"What's that supposed to mean?"

"How many of you are actually aware of what is going on, not only in the center of Mother Earth, but all over in every celestial center in the universe? Earth really is the 'talk of the town!'"

"Why?"

"I was going to show you before you decided to return here. You made that choice. It was clear to me."

"What did you mean about all the celestial centers of the universe?"

"Ah, ha! So you really are listening. I thought I passed you right by on that one." Ty began to dance around her. He waved his arms, laughed and kissed her on her cheek. This was not the Ty she knew, the reserved intellectual guru. He indulged himself in his self-congratulatory fun until he looked over and saw Elisha gathering up her basket and water bottle and heading for the house. He was at her side instantly. Ty tried to grab her hand, but she held it tight against her side.

"Hey, I'm sorry. I didn't mean to hurt you or to put you off."

"You could have fooled me," Elisha snapped.

"Could we start over? I mean, maybe I've been around these parts a little too long, and I'm adopting some of your ways. I should be more direct. I usually am. Yet, these last few days I've been so circumspect, even smug. Then at other times I feel even speechless around you."

"A common problem," Elisha smiled. She was beginning to see the humor in this fellow's obvious confusion over his mission and his feelings for some of the human beings he had encountered. She of all of them was special to him, and she knew it.

In an inspired moment she motioned for him to stand in front of her. She placed her hands on his shoulders and looked intently into those searching amber eyes.

"I'm here for you, Ty. I'm here, for whatever you need. I want you to know that. In fact, I feel it is so important that you do know that, that at the risk of beating it into the ground, I'm going to stress it so we can get on with things. I have the same sense of urgency you have. Maybe I'm afraid of it, and maybe that makes me run from it, but I feel a sense of time crashing in on me too. I felt it a few months ago, but I didn't know what it meant. I feel it now as I walk up and down and all around my kitchen. I can't sleep, and I can't do anything constructive either. I'm a mess."

"You're only feeling the anxiety pangs from Mother Earth," Ty said. "She feels the same way. She wants to act but she knows the consequences, so she holds her anxiety and her anger in, and it is transmitted to all those who tap into her energy, even for a short time. That is what you are going through right now."

"I'm feeling her?" Elisha asked.

"You are part of her, and she is a part of you. How could you not be?"

"I'm beginning to understand, Ty. Please help me."

"I would not have come to you if I didn't already know that." With that he held her for what seemed to be an hour. Slowly they fell to the ground and held each other until blessed sleep carried them back to Shamar, one knowing and one unknowing that their return was inevitable and foretold.

CHAPTER 7

꘎   "Hallo, old friend," shouted Ito. "Hallo, and how is my singular colleague faring on this glorious Chesapeake morning?" he repeated.

"Pretty good," answered Una. "I picked up that phrase just yesterday in town. I heard two men greeting each other. That is what they said."

"Speaking of town," Ito said, "What have you seen?"

"Not much. The high point of the week was spotting two angels preening each other down at Town Dock. They were sitting right next to another couple, a local boy and girl, must have been eighteen years old, and they didn't even notice them. I think they would have gotten an eye full if they could have seen the angels."

"Oh, very public display they were putting on?" Ito moved closer.

"Yes, very. The people down here do not know what they are missing," Una blushed.

"Seems to me that that is the least of it. They know precious little, period," Ito said.

"What is that adage they have down here about dining with angels? They sure are blind."

"No, but the angels didn't reveal themselves."

"Why not?"

"Maybe they're tired of doing it and still not being noticed," Una said. Changing the subject Una added, "I spied on that fellow Seward yesterday."

"Oh, yes?"

"Yes, I'd say he's as good an example as any of them."

"Probably right."

"The other day he exterminated all of the mice in his boat-house. Killed them all off with a passion. You know what?"

"What?"

"The next day, Ada, you remember Ada, she was also at the Council, she directed all of her kin to move from his barn right back into the boathouse. They lined up, and she led them right in. Yes—and she had them chew on every one of his sails. Just a few bites on each one will set him back; that is enough. Do you think he'll know who did it?"

"Him? Never. He'll blame it on the exterminator or maybe his gardener, but he'll never suspect Ada. Who'd suspect a Nature Spirit? He'll probably fire his gardener. That's the way these people react. No thought or analysis," Ito said. He continued, "How will they handle it when Huron starts in on them?"

"Beats me." Una turned. "Uh, that's another phrase I picked up."

"It will beat them," Ito said gleefully. With that, Ito and Una were gone.

CHAPTER 8

Elisha walked into the hardware store through the back door. A black barrette lifted her hair high in a pony tail. Her jeans were muddied at the knees, testament to her morning foray into the garden. Her left sandal sole caught the door sill, and she fell forward crashing into the metal shelves full of exterior house paint. Down she went together with a dozen cans; none opened; that was lucky.

"Hey, nice way to make an entrance," I grinned as I picked her up off the floor. Rushing to her rescue made me feel good. I had some value to her. It's true, Ty may be able to sweep her off her feet, but there is still room for me to pick up the pieces when he's not around. Believe me, he's not always around, and I doubt he'll make a life career of teaching Elisha Martin here in Oyster Cove, Rural America, U.S.A.

"Oh, gosh, thanks, Will," Elisha said as she smoothed out her shirt and tucked it back into her jeans while pretending not to be unnerved by her clumsiness. Elisha definitely did not ever enjoy being embarrassed. In my memory I never saw her clumsy or off guard or caught by surprise for that matter. She was, by all accounts, one of those people always in control.

"Mind on other things?" I asked.

"Nooo; my sandal is just coming apart. Half of the sole keeps bending under the shoe, and I'm always tripping."

"Sounds like it's time for a new pair," I said.

"Maybe, after I get what I need for the house. Now that I'm out of gainful employment, I have to watch every penny."

"Oh, you can't fool me, you still have something left from your parents."

"What business is it of yours?" she fired back.

I felt that I'd treaded too heavily on this. That's me. I never quit when I'm ahead. Around her I say things even I know are stupid. She does that to me. I try to make conversation with her so she'll spend some time with me before she makes her purchases and runs out the door. Problem is—I always say the wrong thing.

"So, what do you need today?" I asked. It was better at this point to confine things to the hardware trade. I was safe there.

"Dishdrainer, putty knife, tomato stakes and two paint brushes."

"Blue, white or beige dishdrainer?"

"White."

"Let's see, I'll run and get the stakes. Be right back."

I went outside to the storage shed. Darn, I thought, Jimmy Wellington always hides the tomato stakes. It took me five minutes to find them behind the lime sacks. When I returned, Elisha was gone.

"Got tired of waiting," Jimmy said. "Said I should say good-bye to you for her. Well, good-bye." Jimmy held up his hand in his weak attempt to mimic Elisha's very demure sexy wave.

"Darn," was all I said.

Elisha did not get far that day, not even to her car. She was careful as she put her foot up over the stoop at the store's back door—no repeat performance this time.

"You're not going to live that last one down in Will's head, Elisha." Ty was there standing in front of her.

"Honestly, do you see everything I do?" she asked.

"Oh no, only mostly everything," he replied.

Her mind instantly raced to things she wished he would not see. Privacy was her strong suit.

"Afraid I'm infringing on places you think I don't belong?" he asked.

"Can't I keep anything from you?"

"No."

"Then why do I fight it all the time? Why don't I resign myself to knowing that you see everything I do and hear everything I say and think?" Her voice was intensifying.

"Elisha, come with me," Ty said as he placed his arm on her shoulder; he could feel her bones beneath her pink tee shirt; she was indeed, frail. "Fight all you want or surrender. It doesn't matter. I'm still here to teach and to help you. I . . . I" his voice trailed off to a whisper. He wanted to say more; he felt more, but he could not.

"Let's return to Shamar, Elisha."

"Ty, you know what happened the last time." Indeed, he did, and she was even thinner and weaker now. He remembered her shoulder and its slight frame under her shirt.

"I bet you can handle it. You had a rough time at first, but just remember to breathe deeply and let Huron help you." Ty was intent on making it happen.

"Who exactly is Huron?" Elisha asked.

"He is the son of the Spirit. He infuses all of us with health and with inspiration. He is the source of all strength."

"Well, if he's all those things, better tell him to pay attention." She winked at Ty.

"Some call her 'she,'" Ty continued.

"Okay, tell 'her' to watch out for me!" Elisha laughed, and as she did she felt the sensation of falling down a well, of losing her balance, of losing herself all in one beat of her laugh. She lost her equilibrium. She fell to the floor in Ty's arms. In a whoosh of air she was lifted off the pavement and carried with Ty upward to the heavens, up past the low clouds, up past the wave of air we know as the jet stream, up higher and higher until she began to soar, arms outstretched, legs aloft. She was a giant condor, an eagle, a swan, all at once, gliding, catching each river of wind and surrendering.

"Elisha, Elisha, yes, you are giving in to it. You are crossing the border," Ty shouted. "You are at the River's edge. Go on ahead; go into it. Feel the water; feel its coolness. Pull your hands through it. Feel the life in it. Feel the energy of all of our lives caught up in it."

Elisha kept her eyes closed tightly. Yet she saw it all. She saw young Elisha, Ellie, her mother called her, in her tree-house amid the Japanese maples in her old home in Oyster Cove. "That's little me!" she shouted.

"There I am graduating from high school with my grandparents and all the family there clapping. Remember, I had a deep suntan; I had been sunbathing on Senior Day, and I looked so good in my white pique dress with the green and pink wool trim full of flowers. And see, there's the pearl necklace Mom and Dad gave me for my graduation present. It's beautiful. I still have it. I looked at it yesterday.

"Oh, Ty, look, look, I see the whole congregation sitting there in my old church. They have a new minister now. He looks very stern; they don't look too happy, do they Ty? That's what they get for berating me so badly."

With this a jolt of electricity went through her, shocking her, sending her catapulting head over back, over and over until her stomach could sustain this injustice no more, and let loose with the worst stomach cramps and vomiting she had every known.

"That will teach you not to bear such grudges, Elisha," Ty spoke calmly. She slowly released her mind, which was locked in old grudges; calm enveloped her.

"That man will bring them peace. He is what they need. You have no right to continue to lead or influence them. You had your time there. Your served them. It is now over. Accept it; accept it; Elisha."

"Ty, look up ahead. Do you see it? It is my little house Whispers. It's all windy; the shutters are banging. Look, Ty, the slats in the shutters are all falling off, and they are all up in the air. Now the front door is gone. What's going on? We'd better go back. I have to save Felicity," she screamed.

"Never mind. You are seeing it, but from another reality. It will come; there's no need to go back there now. Keep calm; keep calm," Ty soothed her.

"What am I seeing?"

"Your life."

"Yes, but the future?"

"The possible future, yes." Ty replied.

"You mean we can change the future?"

"Not exactly."

"Well, then what do you mean?" Elisha was calm now, suspended in the River and feeling no differently than she did sitting in her favorite white wicker chair on Whisper's front porch. The River was an illusion and yet fantastically real.

"Can we change it?" she implored him. Ty remained silent.

"Come on, I'm on to something, I think; can we change it, Ty?"

Ty took her hand and pulled her out of the water to the bank of the River.

"Sit down for a moment and rest," he said.

"Answer me!"

"I will in time," he responded. "In time."

Elisha gathered her composure and looked around her at the sandy shore of this River which looked like most of the others she had seen in her life. The shore gave way to the encroachment by wild blueberries and other undergrowth that claimed much of the land between the River and the forest. The trees were tall and had scant foliage low on the trunks. The leaves formed a green canopy providing cool shade for the world underneath. A mountain lion appeared after some minutes; he moved quietly to the bank of the River for a drink. Soon a gazelle joined him; then a family of brown rabbits, three geese and what seemed to be an array of gray field mice. No group paid the other any mind. They drank leisurely, and some nibbled the new green shoots of water grass along the bank.

"This is not just any river is it, Ty?"

"Nooo. You can definitely say that. Where else do you find this tranquility and respect?"

"Not where I come from," Elisha replied.

"We are in Shamar," said Ty.

"I see. And who are you, my dear friend, a fairy? A leprechaun? One of those strange, fanciful beings who lurks around tree trunks and ferns?"

Ty watched her with amusement. He wanted to dabble in her fantasies, but there was no more time for that. She and all like her had already had too much time to luxuriate in delightful whimsy. Ecstatic play would be fun, but there was no time.

"Now it is time to look a little more perceptively all around you. There is more here along the River than is immediately visible," Ty broke in.

"Where? I see all of the animals; where else?" Elisha turned behind her and moved her shoulders so that she could see all around her. "Nothing else," she said. "I see nothing else."

"What is that round spot over by the large tree on your right? Look, see the tree with the smooth gray bark?" Ty asked her.

"Yes, I see it, but I don't see anything more," Elisha replied.

"Are you certain?"

"Yes, I am cer . . . wait there's an elbow in the tree and a round ball stuck in it. Is that it?"

"Go over to where you can see it more clearly," Ty said.

Slowly Elisha moved toward the tree, approaching it as a wary cat, circumspect yet so curious that she could not keep her eyes off it. As she came nearer, the ball seemed to glow, to radiate color and life.

"Look, Ty. It's blue and green. No. It's blue, green and brown. What is it? Why does it glow? Is it hooked up to something or what?"

Her hand could feel the warmth coming from the orb. She reached out and touched it. Instantly her hand fell back. The heat burned her.

"What is this, Ty? Look at my hand; look at what you've done."

"What I've done? You're the one who didn't check anything out. Forget it. Take a look; take a look."

The orb began to move on the surface; colors changed. Elisha squealed, "It's home; it's home."

"Yes, you are looking at your home."

"I can't believe it. It looks so small, so fragile."

"Yes."

"And it is constantly changing. Look, the colors keep moving back and forth. First parts are green, then blue, then brown, then back to blue again."

"That is the way it is with most celestial beings."

"Beings?"

"Yes, beings. She's alive with beings. She is one herself," said Ty.

"Look, look, I can see North America. There's South America, Africa, Europe—everything."

"Okay, you see all the things taught to you in your geography lessons. Now take another look. Pretend you are doing more than pointing out countries like you would in a social studies test. Look at South America. What's there?"

"I see a large ridge running up the side, all craggy."

"Yes; those are the Andes. What else?"

"There's a large bulge at the right. It looks green. That must be the Amazon basin."

"Yes."

"The rest is different shades of green and brown. It looks very mountainous over on the left."

"Yes."

"Now, look, Ty, look at North America. It looks so small. There are the Great Lakes. I see what should be our Midwest—I guess good old Iowa is there someplace."

"Someplace."

"The Rockies take up a great deal of territory. The land looks very brown, not very hospitable."

"In reality, it isn't."

"Europe looks green."

"Yes, green."

"Russia has a lot of mountains. I see the Urals. Siberia looks green, but Mongolia takes in a lot of territory. Look. Africa is all green, in the middle with huge brown patches all over. And so much water, Ty, it's breathtaking. There is so much blue."

"You can't live where it's blue. And you can't live where it's brown. And it is forever changing. Here in Shamar you see that, don't you, Elisha. You are seeing centuries of change, past and future history of the Earth right in that orb. Remember, I've taught you that life is a continuum; you do remember that, don't you?"

"Yes, I do," she responded.

"Changes happen quickly, actually. In a few years Iraq has almost succeeded in draining the estuaries of the Fertile Crescent; it is nearly desert now. Pretty bleak for the people, let alone all of the wildlife. There is so little land for living and so many of you," Ty spoke.

"And more coming."

"Yes."

"Where will all of us go?"

"Beats me."

"We can't get off the earth."

"No, you were not fashioned to be able to do that. You are here for good . . . something to contemplate in light of all of your passionate engineers who are promoting all of your space missions. And by the way, we don't want you."

"We?"

"Yes, we."

"Something about us you all don't like?" Elisha began to taunt him.

"Just babies."

"Just babies?"

"Yes. You are infants, and you soil most all you touch."

"That's a nice image," she retorted.

"It's an accurate one."

Elisha returned to the orb. She knew she had more to see, and this was not the time to take on Ty. She wished that she could, but she had no energy for Ty's mental gymnastics.

"There's so little place for all of us," she said.

"All of us," Ty said. "Any ideas?"

"Have we raped her?" Elisha asked quietly.

"Pretty close to it. You certainly have dominated the picture. Why not give some of the other species a chance? Why not move over and let some others flourish? Why not get yourselves in control so you stop the killing, stop the destruction, limit yourselves to certain areas and leave the rest alone. Why do you human beings feel you must conquer and dominate every blade of grass, every sea, every hill? Consider what you see here. You can't go on exploiting a finite area. Who's thinking down there?"

"We were told we have dominion over all the birds of the air and fish of the sea."

"Until there are none? You'll all starve. It would serve you right. The Creator would not mind starting over." Ty turned his face; he was not sure he was on solid ground here. The Creator loved this planet.

"How do you know what God would do?"

"How do you?" he chided her.

"Well, I don't!"

"And you're a minister. Break out of those old biblical interpretations. They served their purposes years ago when there were precious few human beings around. They are antiquated now. They were apologies for the rules of various kings. Didn't they teach you that in seminary?"

"Some, but, very few of us accepted it."

"Well, it's time to start." Ty was quiet. Elisha moved to break the silence between them.

"I see. This is a pretty tall order. How do you convince people they are not all there is? How do you tell them less is more? How do you tell them to limit themselves before they kill themselves? How do you shock them enough? How do you get through when people feel it can go on forever? How can you convince them there is precious little arable land for the growth of crops, and it cannot possibly sustain future generations?" She broke out in a profuse sweat and wrung her hands. "How? How?"

"Begin by starting to think of others first. Stop thinking that you'll die if you have no food. Think about how the other species already feel with no food and no mating places. Turn the whole thing around a little. Think of their rights as inalienable, not just yours. You have the same Creator, don't you?"

"Yes."

"Well, start showing you know that. Respect them for the very fact they exist—not just because they serve some need of yours. If you do, you'll be on to something, and you will have a glimpse of how we all view you."

"How do you all see us?" Elisha asked.

"I would rather not answer that one," said Ty. "You may have too much trouble with the answer. Begin by telling people what you've seen here. Don't be afraid. There are some receptive minds."

"Where?"

"You'd be surprised. For now, I think you have seen all you need to. Come, let's go back to Whispers. I see a few red tomatoes on the vine, and I'm dying for some of your homemade sauce—let's just have dinner together."

"Done," said Elisha, and she was there instantly, right in the midst of her leafy tomato garden.

"Ty, cut me some mint for our tea," she said, and the dutiful teacher assumed his earthly demeanor.

"How much?" Ty asked.

"Quite a bit. We're in for a long night."

Ty smiled.

C H A P T E R 9

≋   Normalcy returned to my life as I resumed filling
the seasonal demands of all the local residents back at my central
endeavor in life, 'Campbell's Hardware'. A curious antique, the
local hardware store is the last great outpost where people can
discuss more than their purchases with the proprietor. Indeed,
most of my time was spent having my ear bent by this one or that
one. During the summer of 1994, however, most of the conversations centered around the ills of the Bay and the activities over in
White Marsh. The old linoleum that I had put on the front counter ten years ago began to wear immediately after I installed it. It
was now well worn from the constant flow of products across it,
not to mention the many who leaned on it like an old friend; their
fingerprints like a woodburner's etching had created a counter
of memories. On reflection, I decided not to replace it; it was
comfortable.

It is true that the only place where I can be reached regularly
and accessibly is at the store. Still, I always harbored a sense of re-
sentment that most of the Village business truly was transacted
and required by me to be completed while I was in the midst of
packing sacks of paint brushes and scotch tape for my customers.
On one particularly busy morning, Jason Pratt strolled in and
called me over to the side.

"See here now, Will. I've decided that there are too many
drains on the Village coffers made by people requesting you to
issue letters concerning the legality of various decks and struc-
tures on their properties. I've noticed that you average about ten

applications a month. Your time should be spent on the matters of the Village Boards, not on individual questions, or their attorneys' inquiries concerning code requirements of buildings and additions. Therefore, from now on, you are directed to charge each and every resident for your time incurred in giving out any information, including the writing of letters. I'm sick and tired of the Mayor allowing you to be tied up with these things. Furthermore, our Village attorney is being asked to render too many opinions. It's a drain on our budget. I am charged with keeping costs down as a Trustee, and I'm going to do my level best to see that I make a dent in the problem."

As I listened to Mr. Pratt, I mused. The very reason that the Village had been incorporated was so that it retained zoning powers. Of course, back in the 1920s and 1930s this was done by numerous local villages in order to carve out grand estates and large tracts. This effectively kept most people out, even those with middle class incomes. All of the inquiries that Trustee Pratt criticized were necessary and incidental to the zoning powers, and they were required to be answered by the Village at no cost to the residents. It seemed to me to be a bit of electioneering and short sightedness on his part. I laughed to myself. I was not in the position of being a Trustee; I still had a better grasp of the Village Zoning Ordinance than any of the others, and such a request was patently unreasonable. I nodded my head, stared right into his eyes, and as he walked out of the store, after taking 45 minutes of my time, decided that I would just file his request in the back of my mind, where it belonged.

Within a few hours after my visit by Jason Pratt, Mayor Smathers strode in looking quite serious. He evidently had something important to discuss with me in my not so official Village Clerk's Office.

As he leaned over the counter he spoke in a voice loud enough to be heard down at the Exxon Station, "You know, Will, I've got a bone to pick with the Village attorney. I know he is a friend of yours. And, yes, I know that he is well schooled in Village law, but he obviously has the wrong temperament for us. In a place like this you've got to be ready for war, Will, and you must deploy each and every person in Village government to be on the offensive against any violators of our regulations. Now, Mr. Winston has an obvious problem. I just heard yesterday that he agreed that John Swain's berm did not interfere with the natural water course, that little stream running across the property and down into the Cliff Way part of the Village. You know as well as I, anybody moving even as much as a wheelbarrow load of earth has to come before the Board for permission. It is absolutely ludicrous that we let people get away with flagrant violations of our rules. I intend to discuss this with Mr. Winston's friends so that they may prevail upon him to act in a more acceptable manner. Surely that kind of pressure will whip him into shape."

As the speech wore on and grew with obvious intensity, the gravity of his feelings was revealed in the crimson glow which had taken over what usually was a rather serene face. As he handed me a few dollars for his small purchase, which was obviously a pretext for his true visit, his hands trembled, and I wished that I could begin to reach out to him. He was the only Village official with a modicum of evenhandedness, and even he began to sink into the maelstrom of dissent which had consumed lovely White Marsh.

The afternoon of the same day did nothing for my bottom line. I took about ten different calls from various residents who were all angered by the telephone calls they had received from Jason Pratt chiding them for their various transgressions. He forbade them from calling the Village Hall regarding their property tax assessments, dog licenses, water bills and the like. I tried to calm everybody down. I devoted precious few moments to checking my stock or unpacking seasonal items, which I meant to get onto the shelves. Each resident apparently had been told a story about the other. Things were bad.

Some neighbors, in response to the tales generated by Jason Pratt, began contemplating law suits; they advised we would soon receive copies of carefully drawn 'attorneys' letters' against their adjoining former friends in light of the fact that a fence now encroached six inches onto their ten acre plot. As the Village Clerk, I was required to deal with these issues, and by the end of the day, I bolted the back door, locked the front entrance, shook my head in disbelief, and proceeded to my special place, where I could wipe the chatter and ceaseless acrimony from my mind.

It was a still evening. It seemed that not a breath of air stirred on the Chesapeake Bay that whole week. The humidity hung oppressively in and among all of the valleys between the fields. Even the indigenous water fowl seemed to find summer heaviness too much to bear. They sat with their beaks tucked closely within their feathers, as if hoping to persuade the whole atmosphere away.

The following morning it all began anew. The Village had a new resident, Donald Gibbons, who recently purchased one of the grand old estates. It had seen its day about fifty years ago, and its chipped stucco exterior now belied even more structural problems on the inside. Mr. Gibbons, somewhere in his mid forties, a snappy young doctor from Washington, purchased the edifice together with twenty-three acres of land as his dream house. The property was zoned for a minimum of three acre parcels, but it had long been considered by the Village to be prime for upzoning to five acres. Dr. Gibbons planned to get his large parcel subdivided into three acre lots now, and to hold the lots separately to maximize the value of his real estate investment over the long run. This was his right.

Unfortunately, the intention of Dr. Gibbons to come before the Planning Board leaked out at one of the cocktail parties. Jason Pratt got wind of it and immediately reported to me that, yes, he was correct; Gibbons was not a respectable new resident who was elated to treat his children to a lovely life on the banks of his White Marsh estate. No; he was a developer; he would sell off the lots just as everyone knew he would to builders who would cram in a few more contemporary monuments just ahead of the Village's protective up-zoning. Based on this misinformation, Gibbons was to be ostracized at once, would not receive any assistance from the Village Attorney and was not to be invited to or welcomed into the homes of families of the rest of White Marsh. Yes, even in White Marsh, the land of privileged, there was an ongoing war between the haves and the have nots, the young ones who amassed veritable fortunes at their desks and offices against the older residents who had once had the fortunes but frittered their coins and dollars away through lack of vigilance, indulgences, laziness or just plain thinking that the money would go on forever.

Poor Donald Gibbons, I mused. Perhaps he had something to say or to contribute, but no one would ever know. The doors of acceptance were shut for good. Perhaps he would move out after a year; it would be better for him in the end.

I did not have much time to ponder the misfortune of Donald Gibbons. John Pepard strode in the front door and made a beeline to me. "Oh, Will, you're my man. Get me a few new doormats, will you. Mary wants the good ones—you know—and maybe some with a design."

"Holly?" I asked.

"No, better make it cardinals or something like that. By the way, you heard about my closing, I'm sure."

I thought about it. What did he think I was, a mindreader. How would I have heard. I answered, "Well, no, not really, John."

"Well, listen to this." He started to recount a story and turned, "You sure you didn't hear about it? The old Royce Estate went for $2.6 million, that's two point six million!"

"Great," I answered.

"Yes, and my lawyer thought she'd get away with making us close at 3 P.M. Doesn't she know I can't deposit money that late?"

"Doesn't she? I don't know," I answered.

"Well, she damn well better oughta know. I would've lost a whole day's interest."

"Really?"

"Yes, of course. Well I showed her where her bread was buttered. She fell in line."

"Oh," I managed.

"You've got to be on top of everybody these days, Will."

"Well, I guess so."

He left; forgot the mats too. He would be back.

My life ran more smoothly for the rest of the week; most of the Village complaints were kept from my ears. Perhaps it was because I did not chime in with each and every chorus of reprisals and retributions. Perhaps each Trustee had merely exhausted himself in his pursuit of the administration of the public trust. But, for whatever reason, I was able to tend to my normal chores at the store. However, overlooked in the midst of all of the other indulgences, was the fact that no further action was taken on any of the illegal docks. They were a legitimate concern, I thought. If the natural habitat were permanently altered, it would never return, and all of the exclusivity and value in White Marsh would certainly suffer. I pondered why this did not occur to the Village Trustees, but a person of meager means as I had little influence. I was glad in a way. I relished my free time, especially during the summer months when the Chesapeake enveloped me in her feminine clutches.

Two weeks later I was awakened from a deep sleep at five in the morning by a frantic Mayor Smathers, who instructed me to head for the Village straight away, to have the local police issue a summons to Jason Pratt. It seems that overnight Jonathan Seward's dock had been decimated. The entire dock had been chopped in a vicious assault by axes.

"Hundreds of pieces lying around," the Mayor screamed. "Get on over there, Will, and check it out. Make sure the police get the summons out today. Get after Pratt."

In the spirit of Village justice, it was clear to the Mayor that only Pratt could have been the culprit. He was to be dragged into Village Tribunal, himself a Trustee, and humiliated. He was certainly not a friend of mine, and his actions had done little to endear him to me, but this type of knee-jerk reaction, so common at White Marsh, turned my stomach.

I quickly pulled on my clothes and headed over to the village Hall to carry out my duties. I drive the route to the village so often my car knows the way. It was about six o'clock in the morning, a time when the fragrances of verdant foliage so permeate the air that the memory of these hours stays with me throughout the year. Early morning is a quiet time down at the Chesapeake, as calm as it had been on those beautiful summer nights that I relished.

Mother Nature is a boxer. She's sly, too. She gets you all warm and cozy, feeling just fine and content; then she lets you have it with a left hook—knocks you out—lets you know who's boss—lets you know who's really in control. It's all a head game. She's listening to us all right; She's waiting, she's dancing; she's ready for another quick jab. Then she'll dance again. Got to admire her rhythm. None like it.

I feel the center of the Bay. I see her on her summer days of quiet and freedom from the agitation that the westerly winds bring. I see her when one small swell meets another and rolls over it; no clashes, no increase in size, just the gentle waves moving back and forth in some imperceptible order.

We delight in her gifts in summer. Life around this watery being has to flourish at this time, after all. It is the season of precocious fawns venturing from their allotted turf, spying, seeking out new places to call their own. In their ecstatic leaps are seeds of territoriality and the leadership of a new flock next year.

The queer millipeeds of the Bay appear all along the shores, prototypes of shrimp that have eeked out an amphibious existence over the ages. They are plucked by swan pairs for breakfast or by the swarms of blackbirds that gather in the grasslands.

The quiet is respected by the butterflies whose domains are unending. There is no wind to hold them back. They have the bay as their life territory; they are unfettered in summer by wind and the chaos and frenzy caused when the bay is not so nurturing. Their journeys are shortened by the commanding autumn that rolls in unannounced and puts an end to travels and foraging. The winds usher in a new time.

Do I feel this feminine side of the watery deep in these summer months? Yes. I don't talk to my friends about things like this. These thoughts are reserved for my private moments when I let my work leave my head and allow the Bay to speak to me. She does, you know. She gives me signs of her anger and disappointment at those of us who hear her and know her but do not listen to her. She has her way. She is persistent. It seems she tries to remind me of what I must do. But will she tire of all this? Will she give up, or will she fight back in ways unknown to me. I ponder these things.

Will she always be a friend to me? Will I, in turn, always be the companion she needs and deserves?

Why too, do I feel closer to her in these quiet months of longer days? Do I really sense her fondling and mothering me now at the same time? She is lover and mother to me. I am attracted to her, but I also long to be cradled in her bosom and rocked and rocked. She cares for the butterflies and the swans and the crabs in this way. Why not me? They accept her as both. They receive life from her, and they remain around her as if insatiably attracted to her power and her ability to know everything and to give everything.

If I were to remark about these things to the people I grew up with, they would surely mock me for my romanticism and folly. I know, I have said it before. Men don't think the way you do, they'd say. But I do ponder these things, and I can't help it. Somehow, she tells me it is all right too. She tells me in these days of summer more than at any other time.

I've seen the wintery and masculine side of her, yes, and I don't like it much. Then she howls with the torment of having to be something she is not. She whips up the waters that claw at the shores, trying to get out, to get away from the fury and the chaos of the internal conflict.

The waves eat voraciously away at the coast of rock and sand with a ravenous appetite for all that has been made and born the seasons before. Life is reclaimed at this time. The millipeeds are not on the rocks, and the butterflies have flown south to escape from those jaws.

She is in conflict in the winter, and in that writhing she hopes to return to her berth and her center. I feel her then, and I sympathize with her struggle. In the nights of howling she pounds her breasts in utter frustration. Let the time come when I can be mother and lover again. Let the time come when I can return to my berth and lie still.

My reverie had to end. I turned down the lane toward the Village Hall and I noticed that some of the myrtle were curling their leaves upward; a very out of character breeze blew in from the East. There was never wind in these early summer mornings on the Chesapeake. It was beautiful though, I thought, as it turned up those leaves, almost silver in contrast to the green overlays, beautiful silver fingers, each attached so precisely and effortlessly to the mother branches. Yes, this would be the start of my day, issuing a summons to one of the Village's finest. I wondered if the myrtle had any sense of the goings on in her locale. How could there be such beauty living within such anguish? The thought of those precious turned up leaves remained with me the rest of the day. It was curious that I had never noticed those particular harbingers of goodwill before. Just remembering their images meant more to me than I realized.

CHAPTER 10

℘   Campbell's early season rush just had to live without me one Wednesday. The Mayor asked me to make a command performance trip with Jack Phelps to the Federal offices in Washington of the Environmental Protection Agency. Even after the vandalism, Seward was sure to rebuild. The Board thought that since I had continuing dealings with Mr. Seward after he purchased his property in White Marsh, I would be a good supplier of details, should that be necessary. The Mayor felt it best to delegate such tasks as these meetings to individual Trustees, since this made each responsible for various aspects of the Village government. I had no quarrel with the Mayor on this type of management; he and I differed in his choice of Jack Phelps for this particular task. Jack missed half of the Trustee meetings; he had more important fish to fry, or so he told us.

To insure that we would arrive at the appointed time, 9:00 A.M., the two of us agreed to meet at 6:00 A.M. to begin the trek into Washington. At that hour of the morning it's hard to make conversation with the person next to you, but I gave it my best.

"So, Mr. Phelps, you're now retired from your construction business, aren't you? Did you start the business yourself?" was my opening salvo.

"You're damned right. I started it myself, and I built it up into what it was when I sold it. I master-minded the whole thing. You know, you can't trust anybody, Will, and you can never let the people who work for you get the upper hand. No. I soon learned that trick. Control is the key.

"Money is important too, Will. Just never forget that. The only thing that matters is how much you have, and the only people worth associating with are the ones who have it. Just listen to me, Will; I'll put you on the straight and narrow. You can pick up quite a few tips if you just decide whether you're out for yourself or not. If you're not out for yourself, you'll never get anywhere. If you are, you'll end up living in a big house with servants and a special garage for twenty antique cars, just like me. You ought to come by some day, Will. I'd like to show you my cars. I've got everything from a Stutz Bear Cat to an original Model T. They're my pride and joy. I worked hard for them Will, and I plan to enjoy the fruits of that labor in my retirement."

I was beginning to feel a little uneasy through all this. I started to open my plastic briefcase to go over the file that I had on Mr. Seward's dock.

"Do you want me to brief you on the steps that led up to the discovery of Mr. Seward's dock?" I felt that at least I ought to prepare my Trustee for the questions which I knew would be fired at him by the EPA representative.

"No, you do most of the talking about that. You have the dates of any conversations you may have had with him concerning the permit process. You take care of all that. I'll do the big talking when we get to the hard stuff."

O.K., O.K., I mused as I closed my briefcase. Sure.

We arrived ahead of schedule at the office and were happy that the federal representative was a kindred morning spirit. He was just as happy to meet with us an hour early so that he would have his afternoon to go out on inspections.

When we entered his small, rather untidy cubical in all phases of disarray, Jack Phelps discretely grabbed my arm right under the elbow and squeezed it hard.

"Now, follow my lead here, Will. Just make a copy for him of the dates of your conversations and give him the list. We're not going to be here more than a few seconds. We'll just supply him with the information he needs, and then we'll be out of here."

This did seem rather strange to me since I had looked forward to this trip. I had seen the Village Attorney, Winston, do a number of applications before these governmental agencies, and I actually thought that if I learned a few of the buzz words and organized the file properly, I might be able to do some of these appearances myself in time. I certainly thought that I could also learn a few pointers from Jack Phelps, since he was purportedly experienced in this type of thing, even though he had contributed precious little at meetings as long as I had know him.

Destiny had disappointment in my future. As Phelps had appropriately warned me, all we did with respect to the dock permit application was give the officer a copy of my telephone log. I had hoped that we might engage in a dialogue where we could trade ideas about how to balance the Federal and the Village jurisdictions in cases such as the issuance of permits. Instead, Jack Phelps leaned over to me and said, "Now I'll show you how you deal with people like Jonathan Seward."

With this he cupped his hands and moved toward the hearing officer. In barely audible words he directed the officer to look into the storage of some hundreds of drums of PCB containing contaminants up near Wilmington, Delaware where Jonathan Seward still operated his manufacturing business. "I have it on good authority that there are contaminants stored on a lot over there, which are leaking straight into the river. Why don't you take a look into that? I'm doing my civic duty by reporting this to you, and we all, living along the Bay, hope you'll act on this." He winked at the EPA rep; that was all.

We left summarily, and as we got into the car, Phelps gloated over his recent coup. "Yep, now good old Jonathan Seward will have something to worry about. This will really put a kink into his operations if the EPA starts investigating that lot where he's dumping his by-products. Whether they're leaking or not, it's going to be a tough time for him. I vowed when he black-balled me from the Club that he would rue the day that he did it. This is the only way you can manage in life, Will. You cannot forget each and every crummy thing that's been done to you. No, you live, and you get even ten times over. This is how I'm doing it, and I'm going to make it a hell of a lot worse for him than he did for me. That's the name of the game; you just keep parlaying these things into bigger and bigger problems for each other. If you cross me, you'd better expect to pay."

A few moments later he added, "You've got to have a pretext, Will. See how I have a pretext; you just keep going with it, see?"

I pondered these things silently as we drove home together. I had heard rumors of this man's ruthlessness not only in business but his tyrannical rule of his household. No one was allowed to voice any kind of opinion, whether it be as mundane as planting the corn one day or another in April at the family garden plot or whether curfew should be 11 or 12. He controlled everything; that was his game. The docks had taken a back seat to his vendetta against Jonathan Seward, and I had become only a small player in his overall game plan. It was I who pushed the Mayor to make the overture to the EPA, and I had made the appointment for the meeting. Little did I know that it would be a useless endeavor in our efforts to begin working with the federal agency on the control of the docks. It was only useful in Jack Phelps' playing out of his impassioned hatred for his neighbor. This was how the big fellows played the game.

We returned to Oyster Cove by noon. I was anxious to get away from him, since my disappointment was making it harder and harder for me to continue even the most trivial conversations at this point. I felt guilty that I had neglected my store duties. At least they were as well intentioned as I could make them.

CHAPTER *11*

ᴂ   The moon was blue. I settled myself comfortably
on the uneven rocks along the shore, not easy to do. It's not easy
to find a flat one large enough for me to sit on for any length of
time. There is always one raised side or a protruding piece of
granite. Why so blue tonight, I thought?

"Blue is the color we assume when we come to you." Ty was
there in a wash of indigo light. Darned if he didn't always read my
thoughts.

"Just how many of you are here?" I asked.

"I don't know, really," Ty answered.

"How long have all of you been coming to see us?"

"Since the dawn of time; speaking of time, your neighbor
Seward has a lot to learn."

"He's not my neighbor. He's a resident of White Marsh and
plagues us with his nonsense, but he's not my neighbor."

Ty was silent. "Whatever way you will have it."

"Come on, there you go with your cryptic statements. If you
have something to say, out with it. I'm not in the mood. Can't you
see I'm tired? I'm fed up with my job at the Village. This is my
quiet time. I don't need you or anyone else to remind me of my
duties." I rolled back on my hands. I was cold now. It was time
to go.

"Why don't you challenge him on anything?" Ty continued.
His presence was heavy. I wanted out.

"Me, challenge him? Forget it."

"Why don't you come at him? Maybe mock him for having that big house and all his boats and terraced garden down to the water. The geraniums don't belong there, you know. They're not indigenous to this part of the world."

"Do you really think I'd be given the time of day? He'd call me one of the have-nots, one of those who's jealous of anyone who worked hard and got what he worked for."

"Why don't you tell him you work hard, and if you made all that money, you'd give it all away?"

"He'd laugh in my face."

"Then let him laugh," Ty jabbed. "I am truly tired of your excuses. There is always a good reason for you not to speak out. You and Elisha are on the right track, but you keep it to yourselves. What are you afraid of? Why don't you face it and start calling these people what they are?"

"And what exactly are they?"

"Pompous, narcissistic aberrations of your species. Freaks and mastodons."

"Do they know that?"

"Of course not."

"I'm not a have-not, you know," I answered. That really got under my skin.

"Of course not, but your challenge is to make Seward see that."

"Why?"

"Because he must."

"Why?"

"Because he's in a free fall."

"Why should I care?"

"Why should you care?" muttered Ty. "The EPA guy, do you think he caught on to that sham of a workout meeting?"

"What sham, what free fall?" I said. "What sham?"

"Forget it—you're not catching on," Ty said.

"I am. I'm trying my darndest to fathom what the devil you're about."

"I'm about opening your eyes so you can open others' eyes."

"Oh, am I supposed to understand that? Am I supposed to walk up to Jonathan Seward and say, 'You're a self-centered bastard in your Lexus'?"

"Yes. As hard as you try to deny it, you have to call these people on it."

"Yeah, and lose my job—are you going to feed me?"

"Just wait." Ty broke off and began circling my spot in midair. I'd seen this before. For some reason, I was not impressed.

"So what's all this about a free fall?" I asked, pretending not to notice that he was no longer sitting on one of the smooth rip rap rocks.

"He's flying high, but he's forgotten that he jumped out of a plane."

"Oh." Maybe I was dense, but he lost me entirely. "Say again, Ty. What are you trying to tell me?"

"I'm trying to tell you that he and all like him have led you to a pretty sore landing, or haven't you noticed?"

"I, oh, I guess I'm following you."

"Are you?" Ty asked.

"Well, partly, Ty. You see, there isn't a person around who doesn't look up to Seward. He's got what it takes—the big house, beautiful wife, boats, clubs, millions. What more is there? He's a living, breathing, walking example of the American Dream."

"Dream. What dream?"

"Come on, you know, Ty. You'll never convince me you haven't heard about the American Dream—the old rags to riches stuff. They filled you in on all of this back where you come from."

"Rest assured, Will. I have heard the term. I asked you what dream."

"The American Dream."

"Is it a dream or is it reality?" Ty asked.

"You see, this is what Elisha has told me about you. You always speak in riddles, and you can be damn insulting."

"Can I?"

"Yes, you can." I felt better about getting all that off my chest. Ty came into our lives in some kind of whirlwind, and it was time someone called him on his pompous attitude.

"I'm not pompous," Ty said.

"I do wish you could not read minds. I'm sick of it," I said.

"Sick of it you may well be, but I'm not giving up on you or Elisha, at least not yet."

"That's good to know." I put my head down. Conceited he is, I thought; cocky and self-involved too.

Ty was insistent. "Putting all of that aside, Will, I asked you if Seward was living a dream or reality."

"Whatever you say, Ty. Whichever way it is, it is." I lost interest. "Who cares anyway?"

"It behooves you to care. Since you don't seem to want to answer, I'll tell you—it is an illusion, a dream. Money begets money and nothing more. It was never meant to be so. Money was never intended to be a goal, something desired in quantity. It was intended to provide a uniform means of exchange and equality in your commerce. Sadly, I fear, it has replaced your very souls."

I could see the passion in Ty's eyes. "You've said a lot," I managed.

"Why don't you people seize back from these kinds your birthright to live here in peace? Why don't you rise up and tell them they have no right to think they are superior because they hoard and amass things?"

"Hold on, why are we talking revolution here?"

"Because unless you do something, all of us will."

"All of us—who is all of us?"

"Beautiful moon up there tonight, isn't it?" Ty said. As I looked up at the indigo orb I fell back. There in array were a host of faces looking out at me from the surface of the moon. I could not look away.

"We're concerned, and we're ready," Ty broke my pensive fog as I stared at all of their faces. Their gazes seemed so intent. Then they were gone.

"For the fall?" I asked.

"How much is enough?" Ty responded.

"What?"

"You heard me, I know you did; how much is enough?"

"Explain. We were just talking about the fall."

"Well, has it ever occurred to you that if you experience something good, a taste, a smell, an experience, you want more of it?" Ty asked.

"Yes."

"It seems to be a trait. If you have a great meal, you want a second helping. If you love a view, you have to own it. If you have a pleasant time at anything, you want more of it. Isn't that so?"

"Maybe, but what is so bad about that?"

"Nothing necessarily. It is just that you spend your time recreating experiences instead of looking to new ones. You immerse yourselves in the physical, the material and forget that a daydream may be as satisfactory as a shopping trip. We think this is one of the reasons you have all but cut off your spiritual selves."

"We?" I queried.

"What?" Ty responded.

"Come on, what do you mean by 'we'? Who is we?"

"You are not very appreciative of your guides, you know, Mr. Campbell," Ty remarked.

Why the formality—why couldn't he tell me about the faces? He is tiresome, I thought. Every time he gets me to the point of understanding, he changes the subject.

"The formality has to do with respect. I addressed you as Mr. Campbell. And enough commenting about my teaching methods. I am the teacher, and I do know what I am doing. I am guiding you as well as Elisha. Your culture has lost respect for each other, and as for respect for other living things, well, it is non-existent."

"I respect animals," I said. "You see me at my special place by the Bay. I can't wait for the swan pairs to swim by. I love the deer."

"Yes, yes, of course you do. You love them for the way they make you feel, don't you? You get a connected feeling when they are around. You feel the warmth of Mother Nature, don't you? You get to relax and be quiet and watch dragon flies mate."

"Well, yes. I do."

"You see, you delight in what they do for you, but not in their intrinsic worth."

"Intrinsic worth? What's all of this about intrinsic worth?" I asked.

"They have just as much right to be here as you have."

"Oh really?"

"Yes, my dear student, really. And you know how I know you lack respect?"

"No. How?"

"Yesterday you were driving out to Elisha's, and you were thinking about her—no matter—she is very attractive and you have loved her for many years."

"Hold on. What's this got to do with it?"

"You are jealous of me—admit it." Ty snapped.

"I'm not jealous of you!"

"I know you're not happy about the time we spend together. I know you would rather she paid more attention to you. But, she is in a sensitive place in her training, and her time is mine; that's just the way it is."

"I can see that."

"And you never said a precious thing to those robins who died."

"What? What robins?" I asked.

"The two robins in flight across Jackson Field who ran right into your truck. They struck your door panel, bounced off and landed feet up in the middle of Ferry Neck Road, or didn't you notice?"

"I did."

"You did? Then what was your response? Nothing?" Ty was more angry than I'd seen in a long time.

"They were two birds. So what. What of it? It happens all the time. Some people actually make a business out of collecting and selling road kills."

"You are a poor specimen after all," Ty snorted. "You speak of road kills as you would crumpled paper cups. These animals and birds have souls and spirit guides, personalities and love lives and children, and you reduce them to discarded trash."

Ty said no more. Slowly he walked away from me and sat down on the shore about four hundred feet away. He remained there for some time. No use my trying to shake him out of this mood, I thought. How are we ever going to see things through Ty's eyes? I was trying, but he was clearly frustrated. If I was so bad, think how many others even in our own little genteel community were worse; Seward for instance. Now there's an example of a human being if ever I saw one. I thought about Seward and his red face sitting atop a too tight shirt collar. I didn't notice Ty. He walked farther and farther away from me, down the rip rap until I lost sight of him in a glade of wild blueberries.

Ty remained there in his silent world for some time. I felt I shouldn't go back home without at least acknowledging him. I sat too, staring out on the water, fighting off the mosquitoes and thinking about the robins.

After nearly an hour Ty returned to my spot, seated himself on a rock next to me and said nothing for what must have been five minutes. He turned to me finally. "You should have acknowledged the spirit guide of those two robins, apologized and mourned them for a minute or two. Can't you human beings spare even a scintilla of your time to mourn? More than that, can't you mourn others besides your own kind? They deserve it. Wake up Will."

Another Ty sermon. I remained quiet. There was nothing I could say or do after his letting loose like that, and I was smart enough to keep my mouth shut. We sat together in silence, one feeling exhausted at the futility of his mission, the other feeling sorry that he had been such a boor, so dense, though I didn't tell him. Men aren't used to confiding such things. Men aren't used to saying they've made mistakes. They just think about it, and, believe me they do think about it. I did. In an instant Ty was gone. No goodbye. I guessed he had had enough of me, maybe for good. Somehow, though, I didn't actually believe that.

CHAPTER *12*

⚒ Sleep would not come to Elisha one night in early July. By this time she had settled into the routine which her new life seemed to afford her. I am certain this change distressed her at times, since she assumed a reclusive life style in relation to all those around her, including old friends, classmates, school teachers and acquaintances. Surely this began to plague her in the early morning hours when sleep no longer was the antidote for her frustration and anxiety.

As night waned with the moon only a bare sliver setting over the trees, she awoke without the usual residue of sleepiness about her and decided to find some solace out in the open soy field. The field was home to the many weeds and wild flowers in a glorious profusion of blues, yellows and reds against a canvas of greenery. Felicity Ann stirred with her but declined to leave her perch on the kitchen window. She sat looking straight out toward the field, her eyes fixed on the darkness of the early morning, moving as though following the pattern of someone waiting in that field. Felicity watched a drama unfolding with numerous players not seen by any of us.

Elisha moved slowly to the field and sat down on a convenient log. She with her rock solid background resisted the challenge presenting itself. She fought something unknown to her. After all, she was well educated in theology and doctrine. Should she be summoned by some inexplicable force or understanding, this would be anathema to her. Of this I was certain.

The longing deep within her, however, allowed Elisha to take the steps out of her sleepy nest of a bed and through the front door into the field of wet grass of July. The small briars of some of the more nasty weeds caught under her feet and jarred her consciousness for the first time since she awoke. The ends of some of the spines of the briars embedded themselves in her feet, and after a time, they annoyed her. In her slowly emerging waking state she chided herself for not donning her tattered slippers, which would have been some comfort.

Almost immediately after her awareness of the annoyance, Ty of the Bay was all around her. He touched her right arm; he reached around her back to glance against her left. He stood in front of her and made his presence felt behind her. Beckoning her to stand, he caressed her hair and held her hand at the same time. So powerful was his presence that she stopped at once and called out to him, as she had done before in the loblolly glade. This time, however, he did not present his aquiline face, the face she had grown to trust, the face she remembered and conjured up in her daydreams so very often. For all of her conscious wishing that he would appear to her in the now so familiar way, she could not summon him or make known her willingness to have a dialogue with him. Her frustration at this turned to anger and then quickly to apprehension, since Ty's presence seemed enveloping, yet elusive, so unlike any of her other experiences with him.

Frustrated, with her heart pounding, she sat down on the wet grass, cross-legged, as if beckoning her old encounters to be replayed in their familiar way. At the same instant that these yearnings engulfed her, she felt a tingling of Ty's blue light playing across her chest, caressing her, stifling her with the apprehensive feeling of breathlessness and desire, all at once. In an imperceptible amount of time she felt the light radiate down through the top layers of her skin and into the tissues which lay beneath. The light moved out through the lower layers of her skin and enveloped her lungs, infused each working cell of them and quieted their fitfulness. From there it moved and expanded from her chest cavity down through her stomach, her abdomen, her legs, her feet, back up into her arms and hands and finally, in one cyclonic whirlwind, through her head. For what seemed to be no time she felt consumed by Ty's image, his light, power and caress. It was as though her entire body, every cell, every intricate working part of her, had been bathed in his light, and had been treated and washed with all of his being. It was as though he had gone totally within her and held her in a way she had never known. The feeling was similar to other ones she had known in the past. For that time she remembered nothing but the warmth and the caress of his presence. She knew nothing of the briars which were now beginning to bleed as she allowed her toes to dig into the soil of the grassy field beneath her.

As she became more conscious of her discomfort, the tingling and warmth which invaded every pore of her skin and every cell of her body began to wash away. She arose and walked toward the house. It was now early morning. Hours had passed since she left her bed, and yet it seemed that she experienced Ty's presence for only a brief interlude. Slowly she made her way up the steps of the bungalow and into her rocker where she sat for the rest of the day. The field still beckoned to her, but she felt no anxiety or passion. Gone were those nagging feelings and restlessness.

The hours washed one into the other as she sat thoughtless in a calm which soothed every limb, every part of her until slowly she gave herself over to healing sleep, one which carried her through the rest of the evening and night.

CHAPTER *13*

꩜   Supplies were low at the store, so rather than seek
delivery from an unreliable general distributor, I decided one
Wednesday morning to make a trip over to Washington to pick
up the needed cartons of hinges, cleaning materials, lanterns and
thermoses. It was one of those rare Maryland summer days,
which is accompanied by a gentle breeze. There is usually no
breeze during the dog days of summer on the Bay. This was one
of those special times when the Arctic cool dipped down into our
part of the world and soothed the waters.

As I drove back home across the Bay Bridge, it seemed to
sway gently to the right and left. It moved more than one would
expect from the gentle prodding of the cool wind. I could feel the
lurch of the concrete under my car as it proceeded along the span.
I always feel a bit uneasy crossing bridges. I guess it's because I
don't have the confidence in the engineers who rely on their mere
calculations to suspend so many tons of concrete and steel. Re-
lieved as I reached the eastern end of it, I decided to make a surprise visit to Elisha. For once, all of the supplies which I needed
were easily available and in stock back in D.C. I really didn't want
to go back to the store for the rest of the afternoon.

As I pulled my car up to the front of Whispers, I announced
my arrival with a gentle honk on the horn. No response. I found
Elisha around back tending to her small patch of garden vegeta-
bles and mint. I watched her work, unaware that she had a guest.
She went about her tasks with a serenity that I had not often seen
in her. Most people would find the work that she was doing

around Whispers extremely mundane and boring. She threw herself into it with an uncommon zest, trimming the seeded heads from the mint and tying up the bedraggled tomatoes. I startled her as I moved closer, and when she felt my presence behind her, she turned around with the most welcome, glowing smile I had ever seen in our almost thirty years of knowing each other. Imagine my disappointment when at her seeing me she muttered, almost under her breath, "Oh hi, Will, I didn't think it was you."

"I can tell by the warm reception your old pal is getting. So who did you think was trying to surprise you coming up from behind like that?"

"Oh, I was sure it was Ty. He's been away for about three days, and I'm beginning to worry about him. I miss him, Will. I miss him when he's not around."

"So, what do you two do when you're here together?"

"Oh," she smiled as she finally stopped tending her flora and greenery, "We sit for hours and discuss things, things you really wouldn't be interested in, Will."

"Oh, really? Try me."

"Well, no," she answered haltingly. "Some things are reserved just for Ty and me."

Her unwillingness today to discuss her sojourns with this ethereal beast bothered me, but I let her be.

"So outside of discussing all of these wild and wonderful issues of yours, what else do the two of you do?" I could not believe that I could be so bold.

"Oh, we sit for hours just like any other normal couple would." Normal couple, I mused. So it would seem that Elisha truly was delusional, or I was impenetrably closed and blocked about the possibility of such things.

"I've come to understand quite a lot Will, in this short month since I've been back. I think my eyes have been opened more than they were in the past ten years of work out in the Midwest. Ty has explained a lot to me, but has left more unsaid. He's come to me for a reason. For now, he is really just opening my eyes to the way things are right around us, or around the cabin here, for example, or the Bay, or White Marsh."

By now Elisha's words came quickly, cascading one over another. There was a power about what she knew, and this was clear every time she spoke about Ty. I had a distinct feeling that the excitement she felt had as much to do with real feelings for this creature, as with the information he was giving her.

"Did you ever wonder, Will, why when you see all of the geese, whether migrating to or away from us, and farther south in the autumn, about their perfect formations? Didn't it ever bewilder you the way fish swim in schools and turn, each at the very same moment and in the same direction, when responding to some stimulus? Why in the world don't they knock into each other and collide, and why do the birds hold their even spaces when they fly in flocks? Didn't you ever wonder about these things, Will?"

I was silent. I remembered what Ty told me some days ago; it all seemed clearer.

"They have a form of communication among each other, and all other beings all at once. They also have a Spirit, call it a god, who guides them. Each species of life has this guide, who protects them as much as natural law will allow. When the fish move in schools, they adhere to the natural rules which govern them. If you notice, they don't bump into each other, and if they did, they wouldn't snap the tail off the one they just ran into. They live in harmony and in balance. That's the way everything was meant to exist. They want no more than they can have, and they need no more than what is given them."

I thought of Mr. Pepard and his boorishness in front of me the last days. The fish were far above him in their ability to deal with their own society in an evenhanded manner. No tailbiting, no recriminations if one got out of line, just a calm signal. A lesson of some type. How civilized in the watery deep.

"There is a natural harmony in all nature which traces its way back to the central life-giving Creator God."

I knew at some point she would bring God into all this. All the ministers I know feel constrained to constantly mention the word, as if to magically jar their listeners into some holy order. It seems to me that it doesn't work and turns most people off. Elisha continued, paying very little attention to me.

"Honestly, Will, it's important for all of us to understand that there are beings at work all around us who are exercising dominion over all of the living things on this planet, including the rocks, the sand, granite and all other minerals. Each works together in consort with the Creator, and each is presently consumed with regret for the way in which the human species has assumed a superiority and unintelligent control. I guess it all boils down to respect, Will, respect for each and every being of creation and the understanding that cohabitation was what God intended.

"This is what Christ came to teach, but I am being shown how his message went unheeded. As a minister this is what disturbs me the most. He did not come to supplant one political organization for another. He didn't come so that edifices and churches would be erected in his honor. He came only to teach us about the rules of cooperation and respect among each other and between each and every being. There are things that Ty is teaching me that I wouldn't even mention to you because I know you're not ready, and you probably never will be ready to hear them."

I glanced at my watch and realized that I had only a half hour to get back to the store to close it down for the day. I bid her a quick but warm good-bye and left, my head reeling from some of her discussion.

As luck would have it, I was jarred from my thoughts when I found an unusual number of telephone messages awaiting me, most of them not involving the hardware store business, but coming mainly from the illustrious Trustees of White Marsh. On such a beautiful day they chose not to play hooky from their jobs or their Village duties to take in Nature's cool and refreshing breezes afforded so very few in this world. They had again seized the moment to focus on their real concerns.

Jason Pratt decided to fire the Village Attorney, since Winston had had a meeting with an attorney for a resident living in White Marsh, who had a question about whether an addition to his house would lie too close to the high water mark of the Bay. Pratt's criticisms of the Village Attorney centered around his giving too much time to questions of the residents.

Then there was another message that the Mayor was incensed at Winston's firing, and he threatened to place another candidate in direct opposition to Pratt in the up-coming election. Two other Trustees called in to give their support to the Mayor's proposal, and it seemed that we had a civil war on our hands in a community of two hundred. One other message had been scrawled for me by someone around 3:00 P.M. I could hardly make it out because it was written on the back of an old receipt. As far as I could make out, good old Seward wanted me—said he needed to talk to me. I'd get to him. Yes, I was glad to have had a few hours away from this place.

As I turned the key in the dead bolt to lock my tidy store for the evening, Ty returned to his lady love. Elisha had resumed her outdoor work, since it took her mind off the matters which were troubling her. He drifted back to her, and without her being aware at first, he encircled her with tendrils of gossamer softness. She fell back into his arms with the comfort and relaxation of someone who had known a love for many years. He held her suspended in this radiance for moments which keep her drifting ever so lightly in thoughts of nothing, just the calm presence that Ty always brought to her. Slowly he began to assume the shape she had come to know so very well, the long flaxen hair and soft loving yellow eyes. He pulled her close to him and kissed her and held her effortlessly for some hours.

He did not become part of her heart this time. He merely held her in his arms in an effort to calm her of her longing for

him and the fact that he had been away for days. Ty had summoned her back to Oyster Cove for his reasons, but he had not
contemplated that he would fall in love with her. This he had
done though, and in deliberate unabashed fashion he told her so
that night. He was unaccustomed to the duties which the Creator
had delegated to him this time. He had not had such a mission
since he had ministered to the one who ate of honey and locusts.
That had been a difficult task; this new one in 1994 was now
made all the more painful because, as he held her in his intense
light, so strong was her love and so open her heart that for the
first time in eons, Ty felt and gave back human love.

CHAPTER *14*

Elisha enjoyed an early morning breakfast and coffee on her porch some days after her last meeting with her unorthodox love. The field before her was arrayed in wild profusion with the flowers of all of Nature's usual cast-offs. Many were just opening their blooms to the warm rays of the early morning sun. Overnight they had closed into their fetal buds to protect them against the slight chill, which was always there as a contrast to the warm, fading summer sunlight. She played over and over in her mind the events of that last very special encounter.

As she turned back to her cereal, she was startled to see Ty sitting calmly beside her, this time in his physical form. A bit shy at seeing him after their recent sojourn together and her unbridled display of affection, she avoided the gaze of his amber eyes.

"You don't have to feel uncomfortable with me, Elisha," came the gentle words. He was serene, calm.

"Oh, I know that, Ty. You startled me at first, seeing you sitting there all of a sudden, and I've been thinking about you since the last time we were together."

"I know. I know all of your thoughts and how they are transporting you away most of the time. However, not to diminish the importance of those feelings, I want to focus on some pressing matters."

"What could be more pressing than this feeling that I have which makes me so listless and removes any thoughts from my mind other than thoughts of you for most of my day? What could be so urgent that I shouldn't be concerned that I'm falling deeply in love with a being that, admittedly, and I think you'll admit this, Ty, is not of this world?"

"Well, just to clarify matters a bit, Elisha, I am of this world. However, I will admit to you that I am different from you and the rest of your kind here." Brushing by this abruptly, Ty tried to draw her back.

"Still, Elisha, I've started revealing things to you, but I think you are ready for more, and I thought today would be as good a day as any."

"I thought today would be a nice one to just go romping though that field. Yes, I think I would like that very much," she added.

Ty pretended not to hear the anticipation in her voice. He had no trouble seeing her thoughts, but he put these aside. He had his own ideas about their agenda together this morning. He began quietly, "Why do you think your church was diminishing to just the members who had been there for over thirty years or more? Why do you think your congregation presented to you an over-whelming gray cast? Most of them were white-haired, were they not, Elisha? Were there any new members coming to hear you preach, or perhaps coming to any kind of fellowship meeting that you may have been holding?" Elisha began to feel a bit uneasy at all these questions.

"How do you know the age of my members, and how do you know they stopped coming, and what does that mean anyway?"

"Don't get defensive, Elisha. This is not an attack on you. I am trying to make a point through an example which you should easily understand. There were no young people, were there?"

"No," she answered.

"And there were no free spirited thinkers either, were there? The parishioners looked forward to singing the same hymn, probably no longer hearing the words. They never even sang out with any gusto, did they, Elisha?"

"Well, there were times when I found myself almost wishing I had a conductor's baton so that I could keep the tempo going, and maybe even I could feel something coming back from those hymns."

Ty smiled. He saw that he was beginning to break through her resistance to any criticism about her past.

"There is no longer any inspiration there, Elisha. As strange as it may seem, there are many people who are discontented with the spiritual level of most churches these days. They question the ability of the doctrine to speak to the issues at hand. They cannot be uplifted by the hymns. They find no counsel and assistance to deal with their problems. We have observed this."

"Who is the we?" Elisha lurched back. "Who is the we, Ty? You know, you seem to speak to me in riddles most of the time. You never tell me what is really on your mind."

"Settle down Elisha," snapped Ty, in one of the first exhibitions she had seen of even a modicum of a lack of patience on his part.

Ty continued, "There is a great ground swell in your country and in the rest of the world which concerns itself with the pollution of your air and your water and your soil. Pollution and the presence of chemicals and other harmful agents is not the real ill. Indeed, there are powers that can clean pollution, even remove nuclear pollution in an instant. They are available but can come no closer to this planet until there is a renaissance of thought. Many of your people bemoan the contamination, and they question why the Church does not address these issues more directly. There are others out there, Elisha, and they are waiting to show you all how to deal with these problems. However, there can be no intercession from without to assist you until changes begin, and the attitudes of the inhabitants of this planet become more in tune with the rest of their neighbors."

Elisha was puzzled now. What did he mean by intercession from without? "Please be clearer, Ty! Please don't talk in riddles anymore." She spoke plaintively now.

"The earthly peoples have not learned that they, as well as all other matter, are composed of an energy source, which has in common the energy source of the universe. This energy has yet to be detected by your scientists. They are making some break-throughs, but they have not come close to the reality of the makeup of your particular world. We have given some of the physicists credit for their advances, but they have been slow in coming.

"The thoughts generated by each and every human being contain elements of positive and negative transfers of energy. The energy cannot be destroyed. If you follow this to its logical con-clusion, then the energy does collect someplace. That would mean that negative as well as positive energy collects. What has happened in your world is that people have sunk to the constant emission of negative energy. They lash out at each other for no reason. There is no holding themselves in check. This problem is endemic from the family unit up through the nations of your world. This negativity is collecting and is causing a strain on the planet as a whole. It is felt in the heart of Mother Earth, and she will react to this in times to come.

"You had great sages in the past who predicted various changes in the planet, such as shifting of the poles and realigning of continents. These things have taken place in your history, and there is absolutely no reason to assume that they will not occur again and again. They are more then seismic eruptions and movements of the earth's crust around plates that have formed. They are responses to the collection of energy which engulfs the earth. We would all like to help you begin to harness this strength and to channel it properly. We have even considered trying to show you that the pollutants may be removed by us, but we have held ourselves back according to natural law. There is a natural order of things, and before we can assist you, you must all collec-tively start to realign your thought processes toward mutual good and away from personal self-aggrandizement. This will be terri-bly difficult for your people, but it is absolutely necessary if you are to receive assistance from outside and if you are to continue on as a species.

"There are things I wish I could confide in you about reactions on our part to the emissions of your negative instincts, but I feel that at this point I cannot reveal all the facts at my disposal. Suffice it to say, the charges of emotion encircling your planet are far more intense than your ozone layer or your cloud blanket. You have a layer of horrendous thoughts and feelings enveloping the earth, and these are starting to permeate the spatial expanse and are being received by other beings on other planets. These other beings have learned to abide by natural law, and there are a myriad of posited reactions to the present situation here on earth. There are many who would assist Mother Earth in merely shaking all of you off, and they encourage various Nature Spirits to facilitate this. However, they are held in check by the Creator, by the God which you as well as other religions worship. This God admonishes us to try to teach you from within, to show you what is expected of each and every one of you, if you are to live in harmony with yourselves and with the rest of the beings inhabiting this entire universe.

"You know, the majority of your population does not even acknowledge that you are visited by physical beings from other planets. Even though their physical ships appear in your night skies, they have been rationalized in every way possible by most everyone to be figments of peoples' imaginations. We do not have to use ships to travel. They have appeared in an effort to jar your consciousness to have you realize that you are not the 'lord of the dominion' which you call this universe. You are far from being the only intelligent beings within this cosmos. It never ceases to amaze us how quickly you write off the manifestations of these facts."

With this, he shook his head and lapsed into his own private thoughts on the matter. This particular issue bothered him very, very much.

"Come on, Ty. You must understand that a lot of this is just absolutely above me. What am I supposed to do with all of this information, and what relevance does it have to me anyway?"

"I am giving you facts, Elisha," he answered. "I am giving you information so that when things are revealed to you, you will understand them. There is such order in the universe. It is mind boggling, Elisha. It is beautiful to think that there truly is a Creator God who loves each and every element here on earth, and everywhere. There are beings too, who love you all very much and are endeavoring to work with you to help you find resolutions to the problems which plague you today."

Ty continued on and on. At first, he lectured about the discharges of energy, how they can be measured, how they are monitored and processed by plants and animals on earth. He spoke of eons and arphons. Elisha began to lapse into a lethargic state of non-listening. Ty was forgetting his audience, and Elisha's fidgeting jarred him back into a more realistic approach for her.

"I'm sorry, Elisha. For a few moments I forgot that all of these things are new to you."

"New to me," she laughed. "Come on, Ty, I'm more receptive than most, but all this is more than any human can absorb in one sitting."

"But you are to be a teacher," he replied slowly and quietly.

"I am not sure that I am the one to teach anyone these things. I must admit that I've heard your arguments, but I don't know how they fit into our world at hand. The whole thing sounds so fantastic that if I were to preach something like this, I would be run out of town and called a mad woman."

Ty was quiet for some time. "Just remember some of these things. Hold onto them, and things will be revealed to you. That is all I will tell you for now. I think we are both a little tired."

"I know I am," Elisha answered back. "To think that I had in mind a glorious summer day spent sunning and playfully jousting. You have managed to remove some of that zest after all of this heaviness, Ty."

"I didn't mean to do that, Elisha, but my mission required that."

"Mission. What mission?" she asked. Ty was silent. "Come on, Ty, what did you mean by mission?"

Ty responded no more. He took her hand and walked her down the steps out to the field where she had longingly wanted to frolic hours before. He picked a dandelion and held it up to her. She drank in its distinctive pungent scent as it tickled her nose with the pollen lying on the tender ends of its blossom's fronds.

"You are beautiful. I had no idea you would be so beautiful."

"See, there you go again. What do you mean you had no idea? Why can't you be honest with me?"

"Honest? I have been more honest with you than any of your teachers at seminary ever were to you. I am more honest than any of your best friends, your parents or anyone else you've ever met. Come on, let's walk. Let's just take in everything around us for now."

Slowly his arm encircled her, and she fell into as him they walked for hours drinking in the mid-afternoon sunshine. The field looked different now with all the blossoms wide open, embracing the warmth of the Chesapeake sun.

"It looks different almost every hour doesn't it, Ty?" questioned Elisha.

"Elisha, it is so different each and every millisecond that you are only beginning to scratch the surface of the reality that lies around you. But that's enough for now. Let's not talk. Let's simply enjoy this special time together."

And so they did into the hours of dusk.

CHAPTER 15

≈   I lay in bed staring at the ceiling. Time to give this a coat of paint, I thought. The hairline cracks that I spackled five years ago were visible again; they annoyed me. Somehow I always seemed to stare at them, though. That's just the way it is when you don't want to lift yourself out of bed for another day. Sometimes you just stare at cracks in the ceiling.

The phone on my night table jarred me. Who would be on the phone at this early hour? How could I wonder? It was Seward.

"Hope you weren't asleep," he began.

I wish I had been. I would have hung up the phone in his ear. "No," I replied.

"Good. Then meet me at my place in an hour. Something's come up. I need to talk to you."

"About what?"

"Never mind. Just be there. Who do you think pays your salary? People in the Village like me, with new houses that bear the large assessments and pay your bills. Am I clear enough for you?"

"I'll be there. See you at 7:30."

Why, oh why did I have to be so accommodating? Why did I let him pull my chain like that?

I eased into the large pink and yellow chintz chair next to the hutch in the breakfast room. Beautiful room. It looked out over the Bay, and today the room was awash with the early morning light. The house may have been large and overdone, but this room made me actually wish I lived here. Seward's voice destroyed my brief daydream in White Marsh grandeur.

"Campbell, Campbell. Come on in here," he boomed. "Let's sit here in the kitchen. Pour you some coffee?"

"Sure, what's going on, Mr. Seward?"

"Well, now, why don't you tell me," he said as he poured me a cup in his green mug, Lenox, I think. I had seen ones similar to it in a recent catalogue put out by a pricey firm in San Francisco. I figured I'd better concentrate more on the conversation. I felt the attack begin. He said, "Why don't you tell me?"

"What?"

"What the hell is going on? You know what I'm after, where this is leading, don't you?"

"No, Mr. Seward, I'm afraid I don't. You called me here this morning, and I really don't know why."

"Oh, don't you, now. Well, just think back a few weeks. Just what the hell went on during that little trip you took to Washington? What are you trying to pull?"

My mind was racing now. I went to Washington often for supplies. What was he getting at? "What would you want to know about my supply trips?"

"God damn you, Campbell! I'm not interested in your little business. I'm interested in mine. The Feds are crawling all over me up in Delaware. What's going on?"

"I'm sorry, Mr. Seward, but I just don't know where you're going with this."

"What did you tell that EPA flunky?"

It was coming to me. Phelps, his vendetta, Phelps, his few words designed to destroy, his self-absorbed persona—it all came back to me, and I knew I could not let on. I had to think fast.

"What are the Feds doing?" I asked.

"Closed me down. I got served last week. Got to appear in Federal Court to answer to a host of trumped up violations. Have all but put me out of business. If I can't store my by-products until they get picked up, I might as well choke on them. You know what I mean, Campbell?"

"Sure—but I don't know what any of that has to do with me."

"Are you sure something wasn't dropped by Phelps at that little tête-à-tête of yours in Washington?"

"All we did was review protocol and set up a way for the Village to work more closely with the EPA. We've got resources and they have, and we want to avoid duplication of efforts, especially when it comes to the docks."

"You sure are the holier than thou guy everyone says you are. Let's talk here. You know what I'm after." His eyes settled on mine; they pierced into mine; he was on to us.

"I resent your accusations and your characterization of me. If you can do nothing more than accuse me of things I know nothing about, I'm afraid this conversation is over." That's it; I did it. I met his gaze and covered. He wouldn't get a thing out of me.

"Whatever way you will have it."

"Well, Mr. Seward, I'm afraid this is just the way you will have it." With that I found the front door through the cavernous foyer and got into my car. As I drove out his driveway, I was elated. He hadn't gotten to me. No; he couldn't push me around. Yes, and I had played into Phelps' hand too, hadn't I? Suddenly the rush of excitement left me. I'd lied in there. I was becoming Phelps, becoming Seward, all of them; I didn't feel good, and I didn't feel proud.

I parked my car in the store lot and found my familiar back door. I was greeted by the usual 9:30 onslaught of customers with questions only I could answer. I put the whole White Marsh mess out of my mind.

I paid a service call to a customer later that day. After delivering their order, I ventured down to the water's edge. Appalled, I jumped back as if I had seen the preview of my own fate. There carried to shore and bobbing on every gentle swell of the Bay were thousands of dead young crabs. They lay motionless, lifeless on their backs, moved only by the gentle, mourning waves. Most of their tiny claws were wide open as if arms outstretched begging for an answer to their unexplained fate. There were no other fish or aquatic wild life intermixed; it was only a mass destruction of our famous Maryland baby crab life that lay before me. Unable to remain there for very long, I made a hurried good-bye to my customer and sped back to the sheltered familiarity and temporary peace of my small, weathered, time worn, but comforting, store.

The revulsion which I felt at the sight of my Maryland heritage lying face up amidst the cradling waves remained with me the following day. As much as I tried to shake the image of those poor creatures through an overzealous approach to my customers and their requests, I still felt an extraordinary connection with the crabs. Whether this was so because I called Maryland my home for my whole life, or whether I sensed some open cry emitting from their dead bodies, I will never know. Try as I would, I could not get them out of my mind.

Campbell's Hardware, which had so often been my refuge, now began to close in on me. Unable to fight the desire to flee, I jumped in my car and went to my special place. I didn't want to think any longer, I merely lay back and closed my eyes, an effort to put my own thoughts on hold and to proceed into that calming nothingness which I had been taught by Elisha. Even this happy reverie eluded me, but what did come to mind was a discussion Elisha and I had some weeks before. I had not listened very closely since I was preoccupied with the ongoing investigation of Jason Pratt at White Marsh. However, now at a time of great longing, her words came back to me.

"Will, we were having such a great time that day. Ty allowed himself to appear to me in his now familiar physical form, and we spent the entire day walking around the fields in front of the cabin. Will, he showed me every distinguishable feature of every little weed in those grasses. While most people are walking through Japanese gardens and botanical arboretums, I was alive in that field looking at probably a hundred different varieties of living plant life. They are as interesting as any of the cultivated, more accepted plants. Ty taught me this; he let me see some of the almost imperceptible tiny blooms that are born under the leaves of some of them, ones that are normally just mowed away. They were as pretty as any rose I've ever seen. I think perhaps it was Ty's infusion of this understanding that made me see their beauty. I don't know, but it was a great day."

I was quiet. The events of the day took too much from me. She sensed this.

"You know Will, your friend, Mr. Seward, is not what he appears to be."

"First off, he is not my friend. He lives over in the Village and on occasion we exchange the time of day, but he is hardly a friend."

"Well, whatever you call him he's not as upstanding as he would like everyone to think he is."

"He makes a lot of money, lives in a big house, has a whole lot of boats, pretty wife."

"And tries to pick up women stranded on the highway."

"How do you know that?" I asked.

"I was out on Route 50 with a flat when he gave me a ride, and he leered at me all the way to the gas station. I wished that I had been dressed head to toe. He wouldn't take his eyes off me."

I nodded but quite understood what our Mr. Seward found so beautiful. Elisha pulled me back.

"So, don't think he's special, upright or any such thing."

"I don't," I answered. "Believe me, I don't."

CHAPTER *16*

꙳   Evening fell. The sun in her fiery splendor dipped below the horizon, and Elisha was restless. Calm eluded her as she paced methodically around her little cottage, tending to chores that did not need redoing, rechecking items of work that most surely had been completed properly. It was one of those times where tranquility would just not come; her mind raced.

Her inability to throw herself back into life here in Oyster Cove frustrated her. She made no overture to any local church. She was content just to live by herself among all of the wildflowers. Yet, something pulled at her. I wondered how long Elisha could go on living in this time, between the door she closed and the new hallway she had to walk down. The effects of her inactivity and her inability to begin something anew were beginning to tell on her. She looked strained the last time I saw her, though she brushed the whole thing aside, as she always did when I got a little too close to the real problem at hand. I know that she was tormented and uneasy.

Midway between her fifteenth trip from the kitchen to the living room that sultry evening, she ran right into Ty. He startled her.

"Wow, you could have made yourself known to me without scaring me so, Ty."

"I didn't know that I had to announce myself at this stage, Elisha. I've been around here for a few months now, and you never greeted me like this."

"Oh, I'm sorry. It's just that I have a lot on my mind right now."

"I know you have a lot on your mind," he quickly replied. "I thought that I would change the manner of our interludes this one time. I think you are ready now for a little adventure."

"Adventure? Yes, I think I'm ready for some kind of change. What? You want to go into town, or something like that?"

"Something like that," he replied cryptically. "We can go into town, or I could show you what Oyster Cove looks like from another vantage point."

"I'm game. I've worked myself into a slight depression, and I've been trying to dig myself out of it."

"Good. Well, you won't have to do any more digging," said Ty. "Close your eyes, Elisha."

"What? I'm ready to just light off down the driveway. We're going into Oyster Cove for once, remember? What do you mean, close my eyes."

"Close your eyes," he said firmly. "Listen to me."

"O.K., O.K. I'll do what you say." She sat down on the rocker on the front porch next to him and closed her eyes.

"Take hold of my hand now, and don't let it go until I tell you to." Slowly and effortlessly, her pale thin hand met his.

"Clear your mind."

"I've gotten pretty good at that now," she said.

"Well, you're going to have to move that conscious, self-congratulatory attitude away from this exercise, Elisha. I think it's going to entail very little speaking on your part, at least until I get you over," he quietly spoke.

"I'll be good, Ty." Slowly she let her eyes fall back, and she allowed her imagination and mind to drift into dreamy nothingness, that vast expanse where visions sometimes careened across her mind, where darkness sometimes reigned, or the bright multicolored light played just behind her closed eyes in brilliant bands of color. She sat there allowing herself to fall back into that world which she did not trust, that playground that often brought out either demons or angels, conjured up guilt or ecstasy.

With her hand firmly in Ty's, she felt herself begin to rise upwards, like a wisp of smoke. She was still connected to Ty, but he was no longer the physical form which had visited her. He seemed to be a breath of wishes and ideas. He was no form at all just as she was not, and slowly they ascended out across her beautiful field of wildflowers. She was about five feet above the ground at this point, gliding and playing, tumbling and somersaulting, diving like she used to in the old community pool, doing head stands in mid air.

"This is fun, Ty," she said.

"Yes, Elisha, I know you're having fun. Stop for a second. Pick up that corn flower." She saw instantly what he was describing. She lit down and touched the flower, but its petals wouldn't move.

"I can't pick it, Ty. I'm going right through it."

"That's right."

"I've never seen it look so beautiful. All of a sudden I see different shades of blue in each and every petal. I don't think I've ever seen anything like this."

"You haven't," he replied quietly. "You can enjoy the beauty of all of these things without touching them, or without holding them physically."

"I understand." She had never had such respect for the living beings on this planet as she had when she stroked that cornflower and it did not move under her touch. They lingered in that field for some minutes exploring and delighting over each and every new vision she had of the dandelions, the wild roses and the trumpet vines.

"We must be going now," he murmured quietly. "Come with me." He summoned her attention abruptly, and without even waiting for her reply, they moved steadily upward. At once she seemed to be on a moving pathway with people proceeding back and forth beside her. Some she recognized; some were strangers.

"There is Mrs. Grimm, my old second grade teacher, but she doesn't recognize me. Where are we, Ty? What is going on here? Everybody seems to be moving on a long escalator, you know, like the ones they have in some of the larger airports."

"You are on a continuum. All existence is alive at once. There is no such thing as time," Ty replied. "You human beings have instituted that only for your own convenience."

"What's going on here? I've never seen anything like this before." Elisha felt dizzy now.

"Of course you haven't seen anything like this. You are not seeing physically, Elisha. You are living in the second plane which exists right up against your reality, in which you have lived for all these years on your planet. Here is the coming and going of the souls between earth and the plane that you call heaven."

"But why is everyone just moving to and fro, expressionless?"

"They are in the process of reviewing their lives and analyzing some of the decisions which were made during their stay here on earth."

"But I always believed that at the time we die, we go up to heaven, if that's where we're going. Of course there is the other school of thought which would have some souls not ascend that way. Even when you hear about people dying and then being revived, they speak about going to a light, but they never speak about going back and forth on this seeming endless conveyor belt of humanity."

Elisha was speaking quickly now. She was almost falling over her words, desperate to get them across to Ty.

"No. This plane is almost never recalled," Ty continued. "It is a time of learning and analysis. It's also a place where many of the emotions which were set off during one's lifetime, collect. It is a time of self-analysis and the working through of one's choices.

"It is possible to enter this state when you dream. That is why some of our dreams often seem very jumbled and out of place with people and places juxtaposed one upon the other in situations that don't seem to go together. In our dreams we also try to work out life's problems and decisions which face us. The future exists in the past and the past in the future. We are all challenged here to prove that we understand the meaning of eternal love, that we understand how to deal with each other and to give without any expectation of receiving anything back."

"I think I understand. I think I'm beginning to understand some of these ideas, Ty."

"I'm not so certain you really do, but come over here," he spoke as her gentle teacher.

With that he took her, and they glided over to a small corner next to the conveyor. The endless stream of faces continued, but at once Elisha found herself in the middle of a dense forest. The trees were impenetrable, thick and lush. However, instead of the leaves in large deciduous envelopes of foliage which we would expect to see, even in the densest rain forest, all of the leaves were composed of fine needles, like pine needles only thin as human hair. There were so many of the needles that they formed matted leaf-like formations, but they were not of this earth. Elisha's eyes grew wider as she began to see a form coming through the dense underbrush.

"That's me," she cried. "It's me! But I'm a man. A man!"

She could not contain her amazement as she continued to view the fantastic vision before her. The man knelt down and dug up some roots. He began grinding them with a mortar which he had taken from a tiny pouch around his waist. Soon another appeared and sat down next to him. Elisha could tell that they knew each other. They were probably preparing a meal together. The new being was strangely silent as she took her place next to the man making the evening meal. When the chore of grinding was over, Elisha saw the female being take hold of the man's hand in an effort to have their eyes meet. As Elisha watched this miraculous encounter from afar, she stared into the eyes of the woman, who was beckoning to her mate to cease worrying about the meal, and to pay attention to her. As Elisha stared into her eyes, she could not contain what was revealed to her that very second.

They were Ty's eyes, those same eyes which she had looked into so many times this past summer, eyes which she had grown to love so.

"What am I looking at, Ty?"

"You're seeing the two of us when we existed in another time on another planet in the universe that your astronomers have yet to locate with their many telescopes and probes. Yes, Elisha. We were together many, many eons ago. We were very happy then, for we had very few cares. The planet was virtually uninhabited except for about a hundred or so of us. We lived together there in the forest, made our subsistence meals and enjoyed each other's company. There really wasn't much to that particular existence. I later moved on to another galaxy for much of my schooling, while you became more earthbound. I think that what we enjoy about our walks through your little wildflower field is that memory which lives within the two of us of that very perfect time we enjoyed together. It was a place so simple and free of the cares which I carry in my own soul these days."

"What cares?" Elisha interjected.

"You always ask so many questions. If you could only drink in what is around you and learn from the places surrounding you, your schooling would proceed much more smoothly." Ty lost some of his patience.

"I have so much to teach. I was sent here to open your eyes. After all I show you. . . . " his voice trailed off. He moved away. He looked back at her small frame.

"After all," he began. "Haven't you ever wondered about the spelling of your name, E-l-i-s-h-a. It is a prophet's name, a man's name."

"I never wondered," Elisha replied.

"Well, it is time you did. It is a testament to your own androgynous nature, chosen by you before you were born, although you have no memory of it."

Elisha said nothing.

"I know you don't grasp all of this. I knew it would be difficult," he added.

With this, he moved her through the forest and out of it miraculously into sheets of wind and rain. The rain and storm were
so impenetrable that even Elisha, in her ethereal form, could
make her way no farther.

"I'm tired, Ty. I can't stand all of this. I don't see what you're
trying to do, and I want to go back. You're shattering me with all
that you're showing me. Nothing makes any sense at all."

"It may not for some time, but you will soon recall the truths
which I have laid before you."

"Well, start with this, for instance," she retorted, almost
angry now. "What is all this wind and lashing rain, and why are
you subjecting me to this?"

"This is the birthplace of all storms. It is right around your
cottage. It is around Will's little store. It exists everywhere
thoughts are received from people on your planet earth. These
thoughts, usually not for the common good, I must tell you, Elisha, build up until they form the energy which you see exploding
here before you. It is so powerful that it will result in chaotic cli-
mate formations which will then break through from this plane
into the physical and enter your earthly realm.

"There through the medium of storm, it will give back all the
negativity which has collected within it. Nothing that is given out
is lost by any soul, by any element. Matter never disappears. Energy remains and collects. Negative energy naturally aligns with
its own just as positive thoughts of love also realign. Love exists
predominantly. Look out beyond the storm."

With this, Elisha's eyes were carried far, far beyond the sheeting rains and wind which were beginning to whip and tire her.
Out above and beyond the storm she could see thousands of stars,
some close, some far away, shimmering brightly, some mere sug-
gestions or pin points of light. There were millions of them.
They looked different from the starry skies that she loved so on

earth. They were all around her. She knew that she had seen this before, and she felt the comfort of the universal love that existed there out in the atmosphere, out in the universe beyond the planet earth.

"I could stay here forever, Ty. I could stay here and be bathed in this feeling of warmth and caressing peace where nothing pulls at me, and I ask nothing of anyone or anything."

"Remember this then, Elisha. Come. I can see that you are beginning to wear from this sojourn." She lingered there looking out on one galaxy upon another.

He pulled her slowly to him, kissed her, and at once he was kissing her in her physical form. They were there on her porch as they had begun. The transport was instantaneous, shocking and unsettling to her. He stroked her hair for some hours there on her open porch. He felt that he could not leave her until she had fully recovered from this special journey. She looked up into his eyes and remembered the eyes of the woman that she had loved so many eons ago.

"It was very simple and easy then, wasn't it Ty?"

"It is the same almost everywhere, Elisha, except here on earth, but that can be again."

"I've learned so much, Ty."

"It is time that you assimilated some of this and made it a part of you, Elisha."

The night enveloped them in its warm clutches. She wished that she could go back to experience their lives on that planet so many ages before. She fell asleep in his arms with that desire playing on in her heart and mind.

CHAPTER 17

August evenings. What treats for the senses they are! As I got into my car and headed to the Village, I stopped to gaze at the trumpet vines, now brilliantly hued with their classic long scarlet red flowers. I reminded myself that ever since childhood they had been one of my very favorites. Considered by almost everybody to be fence row scrub vines, they tear down some of the precious fences placed so carefully by the farmers. Their stalks run wild through the wire mesh, binding them to that which they invade. They grow in profusion so effortlessly, their blossoms so perfect and unusual. I remembered my preoccupation with their symmetry in my childhood. How could nature create such perfect red trumpets with gentle scalloped edges. I think they tugged at me as if beckoning me to stay and to forego my required appearance at the Village that evening. By jogging my memory, I became a child. God, I wish I could have listened to them that evening.

I arrived at the Village to find all of the Trustees already assembled and rather annoyed. No one had bothered to tell me that the meeting had been scheduled an hour earlier than usual, since each had plans for later in the evening. I fumbled with my files, dragging them out of my old tattered briefcase, which was now coming apart at the seams, and settled in.

The Mayor cleared his throat and called the meeting to order. The formal notice of the meeting was read and legal posting duly noted.

The Mayor continued, "The first matter before the Board of Trustees this evening is the Federal action against Jonathan Seward. I understand that the Feds have sued him for $20,000,000.00, and have enjoined any further construction on his waterfront. No grading, no weeding, no structures of any kind. He'd better not even prune a myrtle. Forget any re-permitting of a dock; he'll never see it. Now, it's a matter of concern to me that we look bad, as we do have jurisdiction over these matters and have to date taken no positive action. I think we might be perceived by the other Village residents as being a little slow to act here."

"Slow to act. You haven't done anything," shouted Trustee Phelps. "I'm the only one that's taken any initiative at all. You tell them, Will, how the two of us ended up in Washington D.C. We did something. We met with a Federal official and showed our interest. I've told you, Mr. Mayor, that I'm supporting the candidacy of Julius Rapscaller to succeed you next June. It's times like this that we need leadership," spouted Phelps in his inimitable fashion.

That annoying vein started popping from his forehead as his blood pressure rose. He got redder and redder as he spoke. I had seen all of this before.

I mused to myself about our trip to Washington, but I rallied myself back to the meeting at hand.

"Furthermore," continued Phelps, "There is this matter of the firing of Officer Johnston. You guys are still trying to protect his job. I'm here to tell you that, as Village Trustees, we can't have an officer who is suffering from depression in our employ. What if he goes off and shoots somebody for God's sakes."

"Now there is no indication that the man is anything but a bit under the weather due to his recent divorce problems," interjected Trustee Jenkins.

"Ah, come on, you know, that's the problem with you guys. You believe all those excuses. You don't know how to run a business. You can't have somebody who is mentally deficient packing a gun around here. Now I just found out that attorney Winston has been negotiating with the Civil Service Commission to preserve this guy's pension rights. Who authorized the Village attorney to do this? It's this kind of thing, this mismanagement, that allows an attorney to run up too many hours at the Village's expense. He's been off on his own toot, and I think it ought to stop," Phelps jumped in.

"Calm down, Jack." The mayor tried to quell the frenetic rapid fire accusations continually spewing forth from his fellow Trustee.

"Ah forget it, Mayor! I'm gonna say what's on my mind and get it off my chest now. The guy goes, and that's all there is to it. For that matter, I think the Village attorney ought to go. I'm sick and tired, and I refuse to put my stamp on any more of his legal bills for his bleeding heart activities around here. This is a Village government that has to be run, not a lonely heart's club. Enough is enough!"

"All right, Jack," added the Mayor. "Let's try to get back to the matter at hand."

"Well, no. Let me continue here," Phelps muttered. "I think this is the appropriate time to bring up the matter of our Village attorney. I've got this vote in my pocket. I'm gonna see to it that the Village attorney gets fired 'cause I'm sick and tired of okaying his bills. How's it gonna look the next time we run for re-election, and the residents find out we've been spending $100,000.00 on attorney's fees for him to go off on a tangent protecting this good-for-nothing cop, and letting each resident run him around all over each and every property every time somebody's got a beef. I'm just tired of it, and I've got this vote in my pocket. Yep. I got it in my pocket."

"I got it in my pocket." By now I was so sick and tired of this that I could have screamed and yet, I sat there.

"There's more to it than that." Phelps took absolute command of the meeting. "On the 'Map of Oyster Point' he has spent at least a year and a half working with the owner's attorneys try-ing to arrive at a settlement on the number of lots to be allowed on that subdivision."

The Mayor interjected, "Well that's not his fault. Every time a settlement is worked out, you ask for something else. Then it goes back to the owner's attorneys and then back to Winston, and then back to us, and we keep second guessing what the attorney works out."

"Well that's our job. We're supposed to be doing the second guessing," screamed back Phelps. "That's what we're here to do. We're sitting here trying to govern this Village, and that's just what we're supposed to be doing. Can't let Winston go off doing what he thinks is best. I caught him walking the property for the fifteenth time down there last Sunday, and he's wasting the Vil-lage's money on matters like this. It's just gotta stop!"

I could feel myself getting more and more uncomfortable through this. I stared out the one solitary window in this small enclosed little room. I closed myself off from the cacophony, and yet the verbal onslaught continued to rage all around me.

I was jarred back into consciousness as I caught my name being bandied about in a volley of words between the Mayor and his illustrious adversary, Jack Phelps.

"Campbell, Campbell! You know, Will, you could spend a lit-tle less time talking to the attorney and a little more time taking on some of these matters yourself. It would be cheaper for the Village in the long run if you just tried to settle these things on your own. Don't you understand that you have a fiduciary re-sponsibility to the Village residents to try to keep costs down?" rambled Phelps.

What good did it do me to argue, I thought. They would say whatever they wanted, and I had little input.

"I, uh, I would like to say that Mr. Winston and I are cur-rently working on a complaint against Jonathan Seward, which Mr. Winston feels will be served on him in the next few weeks. As you know, I did go to Washington with Trustee Phelps to try to dig into this matter a little further," I stammered.

"Yeah. We know all about that, Will. Come on. Let's get back to the issue at hand. You're making too many phone calls to the Village attorney. Now, would you please try to restrain yourself in the future. This is a matter that pertains directly to you. So listen up," Phelps fired back.

Listen up, I thought. Yeah. By now it was ten thirty, and I turned off. The meeting lasted until twelve thirty that night. Strange as it may seem, we never returned to Jonathan Seward's dock again. The last issue I heard was Jack Phelps arguing that the Mayor had been using the Village dump truck to load some firewood from the lot he owned across town. I stared straight ahead and tried not to listen anymore. My eyes clouded over with that so familiar sleepy glaze which brought me calm. I was startled out this reverie by a blue, smokey image, which had silently come through the door behind all of us. Slowly the image materialized, and before me stood Ty. His arms were crossed; his eyes pierced into mine. He said nothing. He stared straight into my eyes.

"Bring them back," he said.

"Bring them back, bring them back where? What are you trying to tell me, Ty?" My thoughts tried to reach him.

"Bring them back."

"I'm tired, Ty. I can't think anymore. If you want to say something to them, well, then just come on and talk to the Board yourself," I thought back.

"Bring them back, Will," and he was gone.

"I'll see you in court, Smathers," screamed Jack Phelps. He slammed the screen door behind him and gunned his car down the gravel driveway, spreading bluestone from here to the Bay and all over the flower beds I had just weeded this week. The Mayor sat with the rest of his Board, head held in his hands. He said no more that night.

I did feel sorry for him, even more sorry for myself. I was tired. I didn't want to think about what we did or didn't do. I didn't want to think about whether I brought them back or not. Back to Where? Back to What?

CHAPTER 18

꩜   Saturday, the Saturday of Labor Day Weekend, greeted me with an uneasy quiet. I awoke and prepared a small breakfast and headed over to Campbell's for what I knew would be one of the biggest days of the season. It was the usual time that people said good-bye to the long days of summer bliss. For me it was a day of dishing out all manner of things from picnic items to plywood and nails for the boarding up of some of the summer places.

As I got into my car, I noticed that the familiar songs of the cicadas eluded me. August had been particularly noisy with both the crickets and cicadas this year creating their high pitched symphony. The morning was unusually slow with very few people moving about, and I began to feel a little uneasy. In fact, I was annoyed with myself for not having planned something for this weekend. There were few patrons; I could have had some fun.

To make matters worse, the sky soon clouded over in what was the rather normal expected Maryland afternoon of thunder storms. However, these had not been predicted. We were promised one of the ten best weekends of the year, and I scoffed again at the inability of our weatherpeople to accurately prepare their listeners. I decided to take a walk down to the local wharf to have my lunch away from the rest of the fellows working at the store. Their complaints of being tied down to the center desk were beginning to annoy me. I was there too, and I wished that they would all try to make the best of it.

The air was still, almost compliant as it hung heavily over the Bay. I had come for relief, but all I felt was an oppressive heat and stillness as though the atmosphere were waiting for a command. It seemed poised, somehow, as if the captain were about to issue orders, ambiguous at first, because the air didn't seem to know what to do.

A battle worn alley cat scampered by me pursued by another even more beleaguered looking creature cat. Why, in all of this heat, did they pick this moment to chase and annoy each other? Wasn't there a little corner of the world for each? I thought of Felicity. She was always so peaceful, so seemingly all knowing all of the time. What a contrast she presented to these ruffians at the dock. They were so battle scarred, missing ears, missing gentility and affection. The contrast said more than the fact that the animal world was varied in its personality.

The swans in pairs glided by. In the middle of their trek between one marina to the next in search of boater's handouts, the male I had come to admire rolled back his neck and gave the female a clearly not so loving bite between the wings on her back. Before long the two were cackling, squawking, and generally fighting in what seemed to be a battle to the death. I had never seen this pair exchange even a dubious glance at each other. Their swimming had always been effortless and content.

Above me some early migratory blackbirds in the surrounding oak trees were screaming at each other from the depths of their throats. Soon the leaves began to fall in the wake of what seemed to be all out territorial battle for the leafy domain. The din was so annoying and the fallout so unusual that I got up and moved.

The agitation all around bothered me. It was so out of character for this time of year, or day, for that matter. These creatures usually had it all handled and under control.

Large drops of unexpected rain soon disrupted my lunch. First the drops played in giant quarter-like stains onto the bleached wharf, each independent and visible in perfect round circles. Within a minute, though, the planks were awash with water chasing me away from my seat and letting me know that my luncheon respite had come to an end. As I looked out across the Bay, watching the storm proceed across the waters, my heart stopped.

Rising out of the water into majestic heights thousands of feet high was a shaft of gray wind and water streaking across the Bay with unbridled power and fury. It seemed to be in all parts of the Bay, and yet I could only see it streaking inexorably toward me and the rest of the town. It was then that I lost all conscious abilities. When I had first gazed upon this wind, not a cyclone or tornado, but a huge cylindrical shaft of gray, it had seemed to be at least two miles away as it moved across the Bay. Instantly I was swept up in it. My head turned over my legs in a long tumultuous roll that seemed to last an eternity. Over and over and over, I was swept up in the sheeting rain and indescribable wind. I was carried up, higher and higher until I could see out across the whole Bay. I could see nearly as far as Kent Island, but that is all I saw. All I saw was Kent Island and no Bridge, no link, no artery, no roadway, nothing, just the water whipped into whitecaps and pounding the shores of the island.

As I turned, I also saw what seemed to be a typhoon in India. Scores of black clouds were coming in on India's coast decimating the homes and people, flooding the rivers, destroying the crops. I continued to turn; I saw the mirages of water that I loved so as I drove down the lanes of Oyster Cove. I was buffeted and turned to see tornados, thousands of them, sweeping across what appeared to be some great unknown plain somewhere. I saw driving winds and hurricanes of unbelievable force. I saw memories of bolts of lightning and thunder storms witnessed as a child. I could smell that musty smell left when the rains drench the hot asphalt, so reminiscent of summer downpours. I saw puddled roads and mists rising from the corn and soy fields of my land. In what seemed to pass in ever rapid succession, I saw storms of all types all over the world, and water both soothing and destructive in all forms, ones familiar and some totally unfamiliar to me. Then, feeling like this had gone on for hours, but within a few seconds of actual time, I realized, the shaft turned to that baby blue color not long ago described to me by Elisha. Immediately, the entire shaft in which I had become suspended turned a beautiful green color, a soothing green, such a paradox in the midst of such destruction. I was still being tossed about and thrust headlong through the center of this shaft of wind. With each new movement, I was treated to sights of storm.

I was the storm. I felt a living, breathing storm of every kind united in this one conflagration. I finally understood what Ty had been telling Elisha. He was the storm also; Ty, the Spirit of the Bay, was a living breathing part of the ceaseless tempest, with direction and purpose.

It was also a balance of life-giving water and rain coupled with the wailing of the merciless winds. There was negativity as well as positive feeling. I felt good and bad forces, death and life simultaneously. What majesty, what balance, what absolute power, all at once. And what miracle that I was swept up into the maelstrom to see all of this, yet I was protected from harm.

As quickly as it had begun, I was deposited back on the rocky shore near where the dock once stood. Shaken and queasy, I looked out over the water and saw the storm moving away from me. Arching above it were the colors that I had seen while suspended in the interior of the shaft, blues and greens, and now yellows, reds and oranges, forming a tail behind it. Curious, such beauty could accompany ultimate destruction.

As I rose to my feet, I saw everybody running towards the water, screaming with despair, in all manner of curses, bewildered, angry and frightened. The shaft of wind had moved right through Oyster Cove, down Main Street and along the coastline. In its path, all things had been reduced to match sticks. There was nothing but utter chaos around me, from fire sirens to police whistles of all kinds. My head ached so. How I wished that I could lie down, but I was carried up into the frantic crush of helpless, frightened people. It had all happened so fast. There was no warning. Their docks, their boats, their homes were utterly decimated. I thought of Elisha. How had she fared through this unimaginable catastrophe?

The throngs of Oyster Cove held me in. As I moved down one block, I was caught up in the wave of humanity moving toward me. I could make no progress getting out of town. I was in the middle of human chaos, and I was part of it.

I saw the whole world in microcosm that day. Nothing had changed; everything had changed. The people were the same; the people were different. I saw around me mass destruction. Buildings which had stood for one hundred years or more were leveled to splinters. Some dwellings which had recently been constructed were still standing. Post and rail fences torn up from their bases were scattered. Docks, which had been considered so secure in their foundations, were dismantled and bobbing in random patterns with the now subsiding waves. Match sticks; rubble.

There was the din of shouting voices, and yet the dullness of absolute quiet. It was everything at once; it was nothing. It was total chaos.

I closed my ears to the screams, yet I could still hear other comments. I saw people holding their hands on their heads surveying the center of town, now littered with displaced boats on their keels, motor boats and dingys all carried ashore, tumbled and twisted among the wreckage.

"No one predicted this. What's going on with all our taxes spent on weather predictions when we weren't given a chance to protect our interests around here. We weren't even forewarned!" screamed one obviously distraught boat owner, weeping over the remains of his once beautiful sail boat. I saw the owner of the local movie theater absorbed in tears. He simply couldn't speak. He just cried and shook his head over the corpse of his livelihood, that which he loved so very much.

I continued to wander through the town which had been my home for my entire life. There were broad open expanses were once blocks used to be.

One beleaguered soul was screaming at the top of his lungs, "I thought that our building codes were supposed to protect all of us against things like this. Where are our city officials? Where are they in enforcing the way things are built around here? I had my whole life's savings invested in this house. Now it is all gone. Now it is all destroyed. I'm gonna have some heads roll when I get the chance. You bet, that's what I'm gonna do. I'm gonna take care of these good-for-nothing politicians. I'll show em, I'll show em, I'll show em," he droned, on and on and on as I moved farther and farther away from him. I had heard speeches like this before at the Trustees' meetings; my head ached with the familiarity.

Instantly, one of Mrs. Smither's little granddaughters, ten year old Jeannie, grabbed hold of my hand pleading and crying, "What's happened Mr. Campbell? I can't find any of my family. What's happened to them? I don't know what to do or where to go." As If in answer to my silent prayers, a woman with her little one holding onto her tattered dress ran up to Jeannie and took her by the hand, comforting her. I knew that she would be all right for a time. Surely, I could do no more for her. I could not even help myself or guide myself toward Campbell's Hardware, its general vicinity or even home. I wandered and continued to roam among the desolation, the screaming friends, the vanquished people that I had known all of my life.

Their recriminations were legion. How could this have happened? Why weren't we warned? Why don't our buildings stand up? In the midst of the mourning and wailing, I glanced to the left, and beside me was Ty. He was there, posed quietly beside me. I saw him, though. His eyes, those eyes held such a look; he expressed the same emotion I saw when he appeared to me at the Trustees' meeting. He obviously felt for us all and yet, it was as if he kept wishing there would be some outpouring of understanding and acknowledgment of the cause of all of this. I could just feel that from his eyes and the way they looked at me. I turned away, and when I turned back, he was gone. Somehow I knew that he would never appear to me again.

It was too much for me. I collapsed right there on the pavement. I sat down, put my head in my hands and sobbed. I cried like I did when I was a child, deep, heaving sobs, a sadness that came from deep within my being, a sadness which I had never before let go in such a way, weeping that must have been there for a long time and now could no longer be held in check. I threw all of that distress out there to envelop everybody around me. I joined in the desolation, mournings, crying and utter desperation.

I prayed for the calm I knew I had felt in the past during times of stress. I prayed for that warm wash of well-being and understanding that things would change and be all right, that as bad as this was, it wasn't the end. I prayed for that feeling. I dug down so far I felt that I could till my soul no further. I lay there in that spot for hours, immobilized by the futility around me and, yes, the pity I felt for myself. I could do nothing to help my friends or even the child who had come to me and begged me to soothe her pain. On that day, I confronted myself and found that I was no better than any of the other wretched souls running around hurling epithets at those whom they blamed for their losses. I too blamed everybody. What I saw in me I didn't like either.

CHAPTER 19

꙳   Jonathan Seward stood on his veranda overlooking the Bay. His attorneys still had not obtained the permit for the reinstallation of the dock which had been destroyed earlier in the season. It was summer after all, and this was the time to enjoy the boats. The larger one was now tethered at the local marina; the smaller cigarette bobbed gently with the caressing waves out on the temporary mooring. How inconvenient it was to shuttle back and forth to that mooring. How unacceptable it was to have to sacrifice at this stage in his life. The death knell from the EPA had not reached him; he had no idea he would never see a new dock; the Feds would see to that.

As he walked around the veranda, he pulled out his pocket tape recorder and began dictating a letter to his attorney.

Craddock and White
Attorneys at Law
2 Church Street
Oyster Cove, Maryland 20001

Attn: John Casey, Esq.

DEAR MR. CASEY:

It has been some weeks since I spoke to you concerning a new permit for my dock which was destroyed, and which is the subject of the investigation in the Village. In our last communication we discussed my furnishing to you the building plans for the new dock. I have done so, but I have received no further word.

You are all aware that the reconstruction of the dock is my highest priority, and I find the delay unacceptable. Please call me after your receipt of this letter so that I may have a full report as I would like to review the other matters I am working on with you.

Yours very truly,
Jonathan Seward

"That ought to shake them up bit," he mused as he placed the recorder on the patio table. "You've got to rattle their cages once in a while and remind them where their bread is buttered. It's the only way to get anywhere these days. You've got to keep the fire under everybody. You've got to hold their feet to the fire. Isn't that right, Julie?" he shouted over his shoulder to his wife, who was busy tending her prize roses. "Isn't that right, Julie? You've got to keep the fire under everybody in order to get anything done." Julie smiled a knowing smile to herself as she continued to clip the dead rose heads from their stems.

"Do you want to go for a boat ride?" he continued.

"No," she answered, "I would rather just stay here and finish up some of the shopping I have to do for our trip a little later."

"I knew you would say no; you always do, very predictable, no fun," Seward added as he sank back into his lounge chair and perused the Bay. He was a bit uncomfortable now. The breeze which had defined the early hours of the day as a perfect Chesapeake morning had whipped up into one of those annoying gusts that scattered the few unswept leaves about the brick terrace in small tornadoes and dumped the flower pots in disarray.

"It's strange," he thought. "They predicted a balmy Bay afternoon. I'll bet those sailing guys down at the Club are enjoying this . . . first sailing wind they've had in a long time. He settled himself on his chaise lounge, closed his eyes and slept for an hour.

Jonathan Seward was awakened by the movement of the gusts up his arms and down the collar of his shirt. As he opened his eyes, the familiar Bay, which had only an hour before been lapping onto shore, was now rolling one wave over another, not the usual pattern of rippling waves, no perceptible order. Just waves out of sorts. He had never seen the Bay act this way; one wave crashed into the next and ceased to be. The waves did not carry forward; they just crashed into one another, a fermenting, salty, sea foam that rose like a blanket above the Bay. The trees were all bowing to a wintery chilling wind that assaulted them. The myrtle turned their silvery undersides to the spectacle, uncomfortable amid the chaos approaching and surrounding them.

"Oh my God," were the last words Jonathan Seward uttered as he looked across the Bay. There was the shaft, a huge tower of gray moving right toward White Marsh. He had never seen a megalith such as this, so many miles high, so alien, so geometrically correct, and yet so uncontrolled. He could feel the power welling up within it as it moved. How could it be, that a swirling morass of wind and water could present to the human eye such a perfect shaft-like appearance? It moved resolutely toward the Village calling up into its center everything in its way.

Seward ran through the French doors and into the living room. All he could think of was running from the huge gray mass. He found his way to the basement, where he huddled with his hands over his head, crouched in a corner while the storm resolutely tore each shingle from the roof and every brick from the wood-framed facade.

The shattering and quaking of the building infused every cell of his body with fear. The death gasps of the construction reached a pitch of thousands of screaming voices. He had never heard anything like this before. Seward placed his hands over his ears desperately trying to keep the sounds away, sounds of his weakness, sounds of his empire's vulnerability. He could not listen as his house was torn down cell by cell around him. The gnarled fingers of the storm responded to no human command. Seward's house was there for the picking.

He thought of his wife. Where was she? he wondered. Someplace in Oyster Cove. She had gotten under his skin recently. He spent a second concerned with her safety.

How will I ever rebuild this place? It will cost me millions. Why do I have to endure something like this? he pondered.

His thoughts were answered with the crashing of shattered windows and mirrors, as brick after brick fell. The house was tearing at itself, as if it played a role in its own destruction. It joined with the storm in the raging dance of death.

Seward pulled his arms tighter and tighter around his knees as he tried to force the sounds from his consciousness. He began to rock slowly back and forth with the sound of the wind. He ceased thinking.

With the suddenness with which it began, the storm ceased. In place of the howling swirl and upheaval there was a quiet, as shattering as the deafening roar only minutes earlier of the house giving way. He was able to find his way out into the open. His dwelling had fallen away from the roof and its rafters, like the splaying of an orange from its central seed core. The studs and beams all held by the supporting rafters at the roof line had merely given away and lay sprawled in their final death throes.

The terrace, which only minutes before had been his playland on the Bay, was now the collection area for the family furniture and treasures. Silver tea services mingled with tubes of toothpaste and clothespins. Seward stood there looking out across the Bay, looking out across his neighbors, who were similarly caught up in the wave of destruction. There, amid the ruins, words came to his lips.

"It will be rebuilt in six months. I have the money to do it, and I'll pull every string I can to bring it back. Maybe some others of these fellows around here have not planned for their futures, but I have. Life will be back to normal in, at the most, six months."

As he pondered the list of people he should first call, among them, his attorney and his insurance agent, he mentally marshalled his list of demands for each and every one of them. Yes, he would rebuild, and with these words he could see the dock he so coveted emerge in his imagination out into the Bay. He would be back on the Bay in all its glory, and his.

"This is a damned inconvenience," Seward muttered as he shook his head. "I had important plans for this weekend," he sulked under his breath.

A sound, a high-pitched squeal, a crack came from above. One rafter hanging against the tortured contortion of his mangled crystal chandelier moved away from its berth and began its methodical descent from the second story atrium. Seward stood frozen looking up at the blue sky now peeking beyond the atrium. He had no time. The rafter struck him with deadly force. His knees buckled under the blow, and his mind went blank. It was over in a few seconds.

An angel hovering in the chandelier crystals flew away toward the sky.

CHAPTER 20

℥   I made it to Whispers some days after the calamity. I got there on foot. There were no cars or any other type of vehicle left in the fury's wake which could be used for now. The walk tired me. I had already witnessed the catastrophe of a lifetime, but I knew I had to make it to my old friend's side to make certain that she had survived.

Elisha was spared, thank God! Her cabin lost some shingles, and the railings along the familiar porch were cracked and scattered. This was nothing compared to the scene back at Oyster Cove and what I had heard from distraught residents of White Marsh.

As I approached the bungalow, I saw them in each other's arms. Elisha was crying intensely, her chest heaving with sobs erupting one after the other. Ty stood there caressing her, and I felt an intruder. I was constrained to be there, though. I knew that I would be needed by her. As I came closer to them, through tearful sobs, I heard her begging him to stay with her. He was speaking in a very restrained way about how he had taught her well, and that if she looked deep within her she would understand that he was always with her, that their love, once declared and once understood by them, would never leave them. I watched unnoticed for at least a half hour while he spoke calmly about their destiny. Had I not been a privileged guest over these months, acquiring the trust of both of them, I would never have stayed.

"You know I must depart now, Elisha, and you know that I leave you with the understanding that only my physical presence goes. Our love will make it possible for you to feel me within you for the rest of your life and beyond. When you have found love, and when you understand the exchange of that energy, it never leaves you. So do not be afraid because I no longer appear."

She could not respond. All she did was stare into those amber eyes, those eyes from another place. Elisha's eyes reflected questions coupled with the strength that I had come to see in her these past days.

Ty continued, "You will learn that the love you feel for me can be felt for all living things, including Mother Earth herself, composed of clay, granite and sedimentary rocks. I spoke to you so long ago about another Trinity. There is a union of animal, mineral and vegetable in this universe. All breed, all emit energy, all exist in harmony, all communicate with each other. You have learned this, Elisha, and what you feel for me you can feel for them."

As he spoke, she clutched on to him more and more tightly. This unnerved Ty, since this drawing apart was not what he could have predicted, that he would love her in a way he had never loved any of his other pupils. With each grasp of her hand against his form, he pulled farther and farther away until soon, he was standing before her.

"Remember, all you need do is to summon me in your thoughts. I will always be in your heart. I will dwell there and give you strength in these coming years. I love you Elisha."

With this he was gone. He simply vanished, leaving her standing there on her porch, her head down, shoulders slumped, unable to move, unable to cry any longer, just standing there. I approached her slowly, and when she became aware that I had come to see her, she stared straight at me. Her lips began to tremble. Through tears that had no end she told me a little of Ty's parting remarks I had not heard. They seemed so fantastic, I wondered whether they were clouded by her unmitigated sadness. I knew, though, that she spoke the deepest truths.

"It's all destroyed, Will; the Bridge is down. We are really cut off from the rest of the mainland. Ty told me that all of the docks have been ripped up, and that the area would never be the same, that it was shattered for a reason. Oyster Cove and White Marsh have been given a lesson, but we are not alone in this. Earth is making her will known, and like fleas on a dog's back, she is shaking us off into reality. This will happen in other places, Will.

"We have only ourselves to blame for this. All of that squabbling among the White Marsh gentry, all of that negativity aimed at everyone else culminated in that storm. That hatred had to go someplace, and so it fermented and grew and ended up in that cyclonic cloud that decimated what they tried so hard to protect. It also destroyed innocent people in its wake; it changed our lives too.

"Ty told me that while you were chasing after Pratt with meaningless summonses, it was Ito who destroyed the dock. Ito, as the guardian of all of the crabs, had made his own first stand. That is why the destruction was so simple and complete. That is why there were no real traces left. But, Will, there are scores of other stands being taken by Earth's spirit children. Ito is only a small part of it. This storm is only one location's lesson. There are so many others; there is so much work to be done.

"It was only the finger pointing of all of the residents that made you pursue Pratt. We all have such a knee jerk reaction, one against the other, that it was the expected response, but it was the wrong one. We don't see the signs around us, Will. We don't see anything. Ty was very upset when he left. He has lost a great deal of patience with all of us. He told me though," and at this point her voice cracked, "That this summer I had come of age. I opened my heart to learning these things, and I would be someone who would bring Christianity into its own rite of passage 2,000 years after Christ's teachings. Christ's lessons have been selectively used for each and every wrong reason, for each and every ego who desired to promote his own well being. He told me, Will, that my mind is an open channel, and that he taught me how to listen."

After some moments she added, in words I could barely hear. "I don't know what he meant, Will."

"I think you do, Elisha, I think you know very well what Ty meant. I think you know that you have to leave Whispers and be true to love and his teachings. I also think you know that he has not left you."

With this, a band of multicolored light formed silently from the field of wildflowers extending out beyond town and toward the Bay, forming a bridge between Elisha and the people she shunned for so long.

I took her right hand and moved her first down the top step and then the next, then the next, until finally she descended from the porch of her now familiar retreat and classroom. Hand in hand we walked toward town. I held her hand tightly now, for I think that even she with her resolve needed the security of my presence. There was such strength in her touch, and yet I felt the tremble of a small girl. I marveled at the contrasts.

I would like to think that I could help her bridge the time between Whispers and her new ministry. I would like to think that she could teach me about the rainbow she saw and the imperceptible murmur of Ty's final admonishing words to her. I am still down to earth enough to feel that we humans can work together if we allow the knowledge that is there for the asking to come within us. I guess it was my old southern charm that allowed me to believe that I, too, had something to contribute to all of this, and that what lay ahead for the two of us walking toward that Village, so needy and so lost could be true to Ty. I'm betting my life on it.

CHAPTER 21

ℳ　September, 1994. The planet Venus was host for the special meeting of the Heavenly Council. To human eyes, the eyes of their large and incisive telescopes, their probes and satellites, their extra-human means of perception, nothing different on the planet Venus could be detected. Such is the folly of the earthling. For on the 21st day of September, 1994 the planet so close to earth was the host to over a million delegates from galaxies unimaginable in the realm of human comprehension. Venus seemed only to be the planet of swirling pink gases, endless sun spots and electric storms.

All of the delegates came to meet there. They assembled and hovered in their luminescent ethereal forms, each being unique to its place in the universe. There was no need for committees to create order in the respective delegations or to set priorities. Absolute harmony prevailed, as each member could read the other's thoughts. If one were required to accede to the other in order to provide comfort or understanding, it was done. No requests need be made; considering the requirements and concerns of the others was paramount to all.

The delegates appeared as wisps of light. Each member knew every other and could instantly read her thoughts. Ideas were exchanged through the power of the mind. To the naked human eye, the site for the meeting was a huge swirling light storm, brilliant in its power, yet calm at its center. Assembled here was the ultimate authority in the universe. Venus was chosen as the site for the Tribunal so that the offending planet could be viewed conspicuously during the trial which would determine its fate. Earth swirled through the heavens unaware that her destiny was about to be decided during those very moments.

Although cooperation and courtesy among speakers was always the unspoken rule, the opinions could not be more divergent. What resulted became known as the Great Trial. Positions were strong, stakes inestimable. Those who had been vocal earlier about interceding drastically into Earth's chaos were even more insistent and demanded to be heard. They challenged the progress which was being made, though the Nature Spirits had had little time to work on the problems of Earth.

Civility was commonplace among the beings, and though strongly committed to positions as each of the delegates was, the testimony proceeded in an orderly fashion. Each was given the opportunity to expound upon her position; each argument was weighed and considered by the Heavenly Council, and ultimately by the Creator.

A marked contrast to the delegates was the agitation and tension among those who were appointed to give testimony before the Council. They remained grouped together comparing their speeches. It was clear that there were divergent opinions from the lively debate. But their voices and exchanges, though fervent, were never angry or hostile. It was clear that all would be revealed at the hearing.

The Council was called to order. Into the midst of the meeting emerged a form whose radiance appeared as a glowing white ember in space. As it approached the planet, it became larger and larger until it almost filled the atmosphere, blotting out the darkness of space, so great was the presence. It settled at the dais forming an image whose countenance was breathtaking to behold with a face full of love. The presence filled the minds, overwhelmed the senses, and quelled all longings of the heart. The Master Creator had arrived.

Soon the other Council members joined him at the dais, and he began quietly and serenely to speak.

"Delegates of the universe, I had not anticipated sitting before you in so short a time." His voice, though quiet, was resonant and clear. "I realize that many of you have sacrificed greatly to come here on such short notice. However, the opinions throughout our galaxies have become so strident and divergent that I felt it best to establish this forum to air your grievances this time, and to make my decision concerning the fate of the subject planet at this meeting."

Almost breathlessly, if, indeed, a glowing wisp of energy can be breathless, the first speaker took his place before the podium. As with the Creator, slowly the ethereal wisp of energy became a form of a being possessing curiously the attributes of both plant and animal. Clearly, he was from the solar system directly next to that of the sun which ruled the subject planet. He was thin with a slightly enlarged head and covered with green scaly leaf-like skin, almost like a pattern of maple leaves fashioned together in the most brilliant emerald shade. There was no restraint in the speaker as he beseeched the Creator to listen to the pleas of his solar system.

"Master Creator," he began. "I was present at the last assembly in which the matter of planet Earth was addressed. I kept my dissatisfaction with your decision to myself, but I feel that it is imperative now that I speak my mind, which represents the opinions of all others in my solar system. We are disenchanted with the progress made to date. We are aware that talented Nature Spirits have been sent to inspire religious leaders on that planet. However, this will take decades, and we do not have decades to spare. I would like to hear a report from some of them, but apparently they are not present at this meeting. I do not understand their absence, since this is a matter of utmost importance, and it certainly affects their mission."

Raising his hand slightly, the Creator again spoke, "Let me interrupt you at this point. I did entreat my missionaries to be here, and I have not had any response from them as yet. I fully expect that they will accede to my wishes and appear."

"I understand, Creator, and I am sorry if I seem overly anxious and impatient," the member stated respectfully. "But you realize we are talking about the survival of the very existence of life in the universe. I respect your guidance and wisdom, your omnipotent knowledge, Creator, but I fear you are giving the benefit of the doubt to a people who will never see the light. They walk in darkness and feel that they are the lords of the universe. You have even found it necessary to destroy the beings of this planet in the past. You are our protector. It is your power which protects the universe and all life within its bounds from the destructiveness of the negative forces. Please Creator, you must now consider this possibility again. Remember your partnership with Mother Earth. Assist her and all of us in wiping out the pollutants which inhabit that planet. I am calling for the total destruction of all of the species who call themselves humankind made in your image. How ironic that nothing could be further from the truth."

"I have heard these voices from your area before. This is why I have called this meeting." The Creator's voice was bleak.

Another voice, "But Mother Earth has communicated with us, and she is impatient with your decision. She knows of the missions, but she feels that they will take too long to have any real effect. She is dying. She is begging for our intercession, and you are neglecting her pleas." Breathless was the speaker as she came from behind the assembly. So impatient was she to make her will known and to have the Creator listen, that she could not contain herself and spoke out before assuming her place in front of the dais in her turn.

"We are begging you, Creator. We are begging you to hear Mother Earth and all of us who are directly affected by the problems there. You must attend to this matter and rid us of this evil. We have wasted too much time already. This should have been done over 2,000 years ago. This should have been done before their minds turned to their so called 'industrial revolution'. You have been more than fair with them. Please now be fair to us. We beseech you. We beg you. Listen to us."

For the first time in many, many eons, the Creater raised his voice and spoke. "Have you any tangible evidence that there has been no improvement? Are there no words of hope for this place, which I have created and loved. I must have facts without prejudice. I am well aware of the biases against this lifeform, the jealousy harbored for its likeness to me. I must have the truth from your hearts before I can consider such destruction."

In a commanding retort, another delegate arose and answered, "I submit to you here, a copy of a newpaper article printed in *Sea Foam Times*, which comes from a little town on what the earthlings refer to as the Eastern shore in a place called Maryland. It details a cyclonic storm of cataclysmic proportions which developed there and the reporting of it. Look, all it is is a hue and cry one against the other that their building codes did not work. There is no real exploration into the causes of the storm. There is no understanding of why the storm occurred or even of the existence of a negative force. It is only a series of pictures and commentary on the destruction as it affects them, and on their own inadequacies. We already know about their weaknesses and their inability to properly analyze truth. Isn't this enough?"

From the back a voice rose. "Master Creator, a proper foundation has not been laid for the admission of this newspaper article into evidence here. We do not know whether this is an exact copy. There is no testimony concerning the proper admission of this piece of evidence, and I request that you not allow it to be accepted."

"I will consider your request," replied the Creator. "In the past we did not have to consider formal rules of evidence, since we all cooperated in harmony. It would seem that this particular issue has created such rancor among you that I will have to follow the strictest rules of evidence as set forth in the Holy Rule." He was silent for a moment and then spoke again. "It is my decision that this newspaper article not be accepted, since I grant your point. I thank you for your astute notation."

"But, Creator, you are closing your eyes to the situation. You cannot rely on mere rules as would these very earthlings in a matter such as this. Have you been so affected by their ways? Listen to us with your heart as well as your mind so that you may take the appropriate action." Juno's voice quivered, and he began to cry. He was immersed in his campaign against the planet which still swirled in hues of green and blue in the void above the Tribunal.

"This matter weighs heavily in my heart," the Creator replied. "When I permitted the human form to appear on this planet again, I had the highest hopes for it. I sent teachers. I allowed their religions to develop around those teachers. We have all at one time or another interceded in their affairs, but apparently to no avail. Yes, my heart is heavy. I have communicated with Mother Earth, and I have heard her pleas. I feel her pain. I am ready to reconsider my decision. I truly do not need more testimony. I see all of you are ready to give the same speech as those who have gone before. I do not need to concern myself with the rules of evidence. We have had enough of the Law. I feel the strength of your collective need, and I accept your desire to have a complete and accurate decision made. However, the true decisions made by this Council and by me are made from the heart. In the end we know what is right. I am weary with this throughout my being.

"I . . ."

In the middle of his sentence the Creator, for the first time that anyone attending these Tribunals could remember, was interrupted in the middle of his speech. A burst of light appeared in the center of the delegation. Its bluish hues cast radiance over all of the members as it slowly materialized into a being. Weary from his journey and from his recent parting, he gathered his composure and spoke.

"Father, forgive my delay in responding to your urgent request. I have been very successful in my mission, as have the other Nature Spirits with whom I've conferred. I think we are well on the way finally," Ty spoke.

"Well on the way. Well on the way to what? You're not well on the way to anything. We've seen this before. You've accomplished nothing!" shouted one of the faceless members. "They are no different now than they were when you began this mission."

"How could they be?" replied Ty. "How could they be any different when it took me time to reach the key people whose mission it will be to teach them? Why won't you give my mission a chance? There are good people who are listening to us, people who will work to turn this whole thing around. Father, please listen to me."

"Listen to him!" scoffed another under his breath. "I hear he fell in love with one of his students down there. It is her life he is concerned with rather than the issue at hand. He has forgotten what is at stake!"

"You are wrong," replied Ty. "Obviously my feelings for my student have reached your ears. She is worthy of the love I feel. She is worthy of the love of all of us. I am hurt by your comments. How can you infer that I would not keep my solemn duty uppermost in my mind? Father . . . ," but the Creator cut Ty short.

"Ty, this situation is unfortunate, and I know you have tried, but I fear I may have sent you on this mission too late. I am afraid that it will take decades, maybe centuries, for the teachings to blossom into forces which would change the thought patterns emitting from that place. I am sorry, Ty, but I must now look into my own heart for the answer. I have heard the testimony of the Tribunal, and I will make my decision."

With this Ty let his eyes drift upward to the heavens where he saw the Earth he had come to love orbiting above, circling this planet, Venus, unprepared, ignorant of this Tribunal, and unaware of its destiny. He thought of Elisha, and his eyes closed. He prayed she slept peacefully. He could see her in his heart.

"I have seen a glimmer of hope there, Creator. I have seen it. I implore you to give these creatures you created a chance to turn the situation around. Look up there, Creator. Can you do what these delegates are asking of you? Can you again destroy them without losing part of your own humanity, that part which you had hoped would evolve in them? You had placed such faith in them. Can't you allow some of your new teachers to create the renaissance we pray for?"

"I am sorry, Ty. I acknowledge your contribution to this Tribunal, but I do not need more information or more arguments. I am prepared to render my decision," replied the Creator.

"Look! Something looks different about the planet," shouted one of the delegates. "Look at the color, that faint rose-like, pinkish glow. Look! See! It definitely looks different. Something is happening." With that, all eyes turned to Earth.

The electricity and charged emotions within the Tribunal were immeasurable at that moment, as all cast their eyes to the heavens.

"We have waited so long to see that color emanate from Earth, but it is almost imperceptible," one member cried. It was like a tiny wisp of smoke rising through the atmosphere.

"It's worthless!" shouted one of the delegates.

"It is a beginning," spoke Ty radiantly.

"Yes," responded the Creator, his heart swelling with love, "It is a beginning."

Somewhere on a small verdant planet spinning around her sun, in the forest deep, a gentle wind rustled through the loblolly pines, and a smile played across the face of one who slept, remembering . . . dreaming.